T0158744

Rosewood

The Early Years

William Garrett and
Rochelle Fischer

iUniverse, Inc.
Bloomington

iUniverse books may be ordered through booksellers or by contacting:

iUniverse
1663 Liberty Drive
Bloomington, IN 47403
www.iuniverse.com
1-800-Authors (1-800-288-4677)

The cover photograph used with permission of Houmas House Plantation and Gardens Darrow Louisiana

ISBN: 978-1-4620-3059-0 (sc)
ISBN: 978-1-4620-3060-6 (hc)
ISBN: 978-1-4620-3061-3 (e)

Library of Congress Control Number: 2011912169

Printed in the United States of America

iUniverse rev. date: 08/02/2011

Chapter One

The year was 1814 and the war had been going on for two years. James Darcy reasoned it was mostly a war between America and Britain. A blockade of the American coast had virtually stopped all trade between the two countries but a few daring privateers managed to earn a good living by providing transportation to whoever wanted to go to America at a steep price of course. Captain Thomas Boyle's ship, the Chasseur was new and she was very fast.

Captain Boyle had declared the Atlantic his own personal domain and sent word to the British Admiralty a blockade was in effect for all shipping. This of course did not set well with Lloyds Of London. James and Marianne had recently married and they loved each other very much. Both of them were eager to move to America and get away from the smells and hardships associated with war and they also wanted their children to be born on American soil. John had acquired passage for the two of them aboard the Chasseur and was scheduled for departure in two weeks.

Marianne was all excited as she directed the servants as they packed their steamer trunks and bags. Naturally she wanted to take everything including a very heavy cedar chest that had been handed down by her mother but the sheer size of the thing prohibited it.

"James, I think it is simply outrageous we are not allowed to take the cedar chest with us," said Marianne, as she looked up from a piece of fine, white, silk lace she had been folding into a small leather bag.

"Yes, my dear I totally agree but the ship's Captain said personal storage space aboard the ship was limited because of the nature of the ship's cargo which the Captain was not at liberty to divulge."

"But most of everything that was given to us by mother and father will not be allowed to go," argued Marianne.

"I will speak to the Captain," said James as he leaned over and gently kissed his wife of three months on her cheek. Then on a sudden impulse he took her in his arms and gently held her. She knew he was not a violent man but beneath his calm demeanor laid the heart of a lion. Their courtship had lasted two years and of course her parents were dutifully shocked when she announced their engagement. Her father was very traditional in his beliefs.

"What do you know of the man?" asked her father sternly. "Is he a businessman?"

"Father, really. You introduced us. Remember at the dance social that was held to commemorate the merger between your bank and Sir Smyth's?"

A look of puzzlement crossed her father's face as he thought about what his daughter had told him. "The young gentleman that was standing behind Sir Smyth was his son?" "Yes, father, remember?"

"But that wasn't an introduction. I merely acknowledged his presence and asked if he was enjoying the dance."

"Yes father but this is a new century. Times are changing every day, every hour it seems. Exciting things! Customs that you and mother experienced will soon be old fashioned."

"Yes, well, perhaps you're right but I will never agree with it. We have to have standards."

"Father, it will be all right. You have taught me well," said Marianne as she reassuringly patted him on the arm. Marianne smiled as she recalled the earlier conversation and continued to busy herself with directing the servants in the packing of their belongings.

The two weeks passed quickly and she could hardly believe she was actually standing on the dock and looking up at the tall twin masts of the clipper ship, Chasseur. Even though the ship's white canvas sails were tied securely to the yardarms high overhead Marianne could feel a sense of speed as she looked at the sleek smooth sides of the wooden ship. She had asked several of her friends about crossing the Atlantic and they had told her a normal voyage took six weeks but as she gazed at the Chasseur she knew it wouldn't take nearly that long for them to make the voyage. She was a little nervous that morning but it wasn't because of the upcoming voyage. For two mornings in a row Marianne had been sick and she knew she was with child.

Her friends had also told her about life aboard a ship at sea and Marianne hoped she could manage. Telling James about him being a father wasn't a major concern as they both wanted children so she decided to wait until the proper time. Perhaps, in a private moment she could tell her husband about the blessed event, after they had left port and settled in their quarters aboard ship?

Aboard the Chasseur a young man who did not look more than ten or twelve escorted James and Marianne to their cabin below deck. Inside the cabin the two stood facing each other and then James took Marianne in his arms and held her for a moment.

"We will soon be on our way to a new start in America," he said then he felt a slight tremble go through her body. "Are you frightened at the thought of leaving your parents? It will be quite a challenge you know. Different people and customs from what we have been familiar with."

"No, it isn't the thought of leaving everything behind," she assured him," It's just the closeness of the cabin and it smells terribly. It badly needs to be aired out but there is no window or porthole I believe they are called."

James chuckled at her observation. "You are quite right my dear. It does smell of dust and stale sweat. Perhaps it was occasionally used by a crew member or a passenger who did not bathe regularly?"

In her husband's strong arms Marianne felt reassured by the explanation. "James have you spoken to the Captain about our baggage and the cedar chest?"

"Not yet dear. I will attend to it now."

James left the cabin and went topside to find the Captain. He wasn't hard to spot standing at the rail by the gangway giving orders to the line of men coming aboard carrying heavy looking wooden crates and boxes on their shoulders. James watched as the Captain directed the men and he had to admit he liked the cut of the man. He didn't wear anything that signified his rank as most English Captains had a fondness of doing. He wore a simple black jacket of broadcloth to the waist over a thick sweater of knitted material, probably twill or cotton and dark pants that came down almost to the wooden deck. His shoes were also simple black leather with a large brass buckle. Even with his simple clothing he was a commanding figure.

"Captain Boyle my wife Marianne would like to have a large cedar chest brought aboard along with our goods on the trip to America. She was informed this is not possible. Is that correct,

Sir" asked James as he stood with his hands folded behind his back and his legs slightly bent as he adjusted to the slight roll of the ship's deck?

"That is correct Mr. Darcy. For reasons I am not at liberty to disclose at this time space aboard the Chasseur is very limited. Even my personal cabin is almost filled with cargo. I am a businessman, cargo and passengers are my business."

"Yes, I understand completely Captain. Then as a businessman I ask if it would be possible to buy some additional space to accommodate my wife's cedar chest and perhaps a few other smaller items for the passage to America?"

"Of course Mr. Darcy. The nature of the Chasseur's cargo is of a sensitive nature, government regulations you understand, but I am sure we can come to an agreement."

"Thank you Captain Boyle. Marianne will be most pleased," said James as he turned and started to go down the gangway to leave the ship.

"Mr. Darcy, I could not help but notice as you were standing on the deck. Were you perhaps a seaman aboard ship?"

"I was. Why do you ask, Sir"

"My apologies for my brunt nature earlier. As I explained, I am a businessman, a privateer if you please but gentlemen of the sea share a love that goes beyond avarice so because of our shared interest you may bring all of your goods with you. Government regulations be damned."

James sensing a confidential nature in the Captain's voice stepped closer and asked, "I have heard rumors of a blockade for ships going to America. Will this be a problem?"

"You are well informed, Sir, and you are correct the blockade is mostly for ships going to America. However, the route for this crossing will be a southern route for the port at New Orleans."

"And pirates, Captain?"

"Oh, I forgot to mention about a personal friend of mine, Jean Lafitte the privateer. We also share a common interest," said Captain Boyle as he smiled broadly.

Once at sea Marianne quickly adjusted to a life at sea. Even the continuous slow roll of the ship as it navigated through the sea did not affect her that much. She did prefer to spend a considerable amount of time topside on deck in the fresh air and even the smirks and whispered remarks of the seasoned sailors as they watched her leaning over the rail because of her condition did not bother her. She reasoned they thought she was seasick instead of being with-child.

On several occasions as she walked around the ship's deck Marianne watched as the sailors went about their daily tasks of repairing the many hemp lines, rigging and working with needle and palm sewing canvas. Several of the sailors were naked to the waist and as they worked their muscles flexed and she blushed as she remembered the many times she had felt her husband's muscles as they lay together at night. She was thankful the sailors chose to pretty much ignore her as she walked on the deck. The exercise was good for her and after a few minutes she returned to the stuffiness of the cabin.

The Captain had been most gracious in allowing them the extra storage space for their belongings. It would be difficult enough with moving to a new country and starting a new life but with the few things they had brought with them now stored below in the cargo space it wouldn't be so dreadful. James was in his element and spent most of his time topside talking with Captain Boyle.

"Captain Boyle I noticed you are carrying eight twenty-four pound cannons but I am not fully familiar with their design."

"You have a keen eye, Mr. Darcy. You are familiar with cannons? Have you seen action aboard ship, perhaps as a Captain or seaman?"

"Yes, but limited. I served aboard several ships as a young man and advanced myself to leader of a gun crew but they were twelve pounder's."

"What was your best time for getting out a round, Sir?"

"We could consistently get a round out in a little less than three minutes but that was for a twelve pound solid shot."

"Very impressive, Sir. The best time for my crew in getting a round out with the twenty-four pounder's is four minutes. If you wish I could put you in charge of the topside cannons. We have a few weeks before port call to get them in shape."

"Six weeks for the crossing and allowing one week for bad weather…"

"The Chasseur can make the crossing in five weeks," interjected Captain Boyle.

"Five weeks to train, four with bad weather, yes, Captain Boyle I will take the job but understand it is only for the one crossing and not a permanent arrangement. In addition I will need only one fired round to get a feel of the cannons range."

"Acceptable and quite right, Mr. Darcy. The cannons were specially modified for me by Colonel Sam Hughes of the Cecil Iron Works and he assures me they will get an additional two hundred yards than the standard of twelve hundred."

For the next few weeks there was a high level of activity aboard the Chasseur as James directed the topside gun crews in loading and mock firing the cannons. Powder and shot were expensive and even a single cannon ball could mean the difference between surviving and death should they encounter a pirate ship. As a final task, he told the gun crews to replace and shorten the thick hemp ropes used to keep the cannons from sliding backwards across the deck when they were fired. Every second was important and even Captain Boyle, a hardened seaman, was impressed with their time of consistently simulating getting a round out in slightly less than three minutes.

From his observation post aft at the helm, Captain Boyle watched as Mr. Darcy directed and drilled the gun crews. Each crew and man moved as a single unit until their actions were smooth and no mistakes were made even using the larger cannon ball of twenty-four pounds instead of twelve. Captain Boyle was satisfied.

"Mr. Darcy, my congratulations, Sir. You do indeed know about cannons," said the Captain as he pulled him aside and the two of them stood alongside the Chasseur's railing. "If agreeable you and your crews have well earned a day of rest."

"Thank you Captain. You have some excellent seaman and they learn quickly. I must say the young African on gun number two seems to be extraordinarily intelligent. Perhaps he could be given advancement to leader of that gun after we are in port?"

"I will take it into advisement, Mr. Darcy."

The gun crews were a little surprised when James informed them they had earned a day of rest even though it was Tuesday instead of Sunday. Marianne was also glad when her husband came below to be with her. She had missed him and was even a little lonely because he had spent so much time away from her while training the men.

"Hello my husband," she said mischievously as she kissed him on the cheek when he opened the cabin door and came inside.

"Thank you, love of my life. I am well pleased with the men and their training. Hopefully it won't be needed and we will have a safe and uneventful crossing."

"I am sure they will do well. They had a wonderful teacher," said Marianne as she looked into her husband's eyes. There seemed to be tiredness in his body about the way his shoulders slumped slightly as he sat down onto a chair next to the only table in the cabin. The day of rest was not to be, however. Topside in the crow's nest the lookout yelled, " Sail on the horizon!"

"Where away?" asked the Captain.

"Port side bow, five degrees," answered the lookout as he looked through his long glass.

"Does she fly a flag?"

"No flag Captain."

Very well. Clear the decks! Stand by for action!" commanded the Captain.

"Well, so much for the day of rest," said James as he gave his new wife a big embrace on his way out the cabin door to go topside.

"I love you," said Marianne as she returned his embrace. "Please be careful. I wouldn't want our son to grow up without a father to guide him."

A look of astonishment crossed his face as he stood there with his wife in his arms. "A son? Are you sure?" he asked as he looked down and very gently put his hand on her abdomen.

"Yes, quite sure," she answered as she placed one of her hands over his. " I wanted to wait until the right moment when we were alone and had a moment of privacy." Marianne's eyes filled with tears as she asked, " I guess this is the right moment. Can we name him William after your Grandfather?"

"That would be wonderful, he would be honored."

"You had better hurry. You don't want to be late, even if it is to war."

After her husband left their cabin she could hear the scurry of feet above deck as the sailors prepared to meet the pirates in the other ship. Topside Captain Boyle commanded the men as they manned the guns and prepared to meet the other ship, friendly or not they should have been flying some flag of recognition.

"Mr. Darcy, you have permission to fire as soon as your guns come to bear." James knew it would be necessary to turn the ship to allow the guns to fire a broadside. It took only a few seconds to add the powder and solid shot in preparation for the heavy cannons to fire. "Fire!" he yelled and four cannons went off at once. The ship's decks quickly flooded with smoke from the gunpowder but just as quickly cleared away because of the strong wind that morning.

With smooth precision the gun crews ran a brush down the cannon to clean it out and then put fresher powder and a solid shot down the cannon barrel. Then a ramrod was used to push the cannon ball and powder further into the barrel until they were seated firmly. A corded fuse was stuck in the small hole at one end of the barrel and the cannon was ready to fire again. Then the cannon was rolled back into firing position with its barrel sticking through the portal in the wooden bulwark of the ship. "Fire!" commanded James. The time from the firing of the first shot until the firing of the second shot was an unbelievable two and a half minutes. The entire battle only lasted twenty minutes.

Below decks in her cabin Marianne sat on the side of the bed and listened to the sounds coming from topside. Unconsciously she flinched each time as the cannons thundered when they fired. Smoke and the smell of burned gunpowder filtered down to her as she sat in her cabin. Then she heard nothing, no scurrying of feet, no rolling of the cannons across the deck, silence. Had the pirates boarded the ship she wondered? Was everyone dead? Marianne was startled when a knock sounded on her cabin door.

She opened the door to see Captain Boyle standing there. "Mrs. Darcy I am afraid I have some bad news. A sharpshooter killed your husband just a few minutes ago. He directed his gun crews magnificently and they got off three rounds before the pirate ship's guns could even come into range and fire a single shot. His crews alone destroyed all the topside cannons and saved us all from being shot to shreds from grapeshot. Just as he commanded his gun crews to fire a broadside of grapeshot and take down their mainmast a sharpshooter in their rigging shot him. It was a clean shot and he died instantly without any suffering."

The shock of her husband's sudden death caused her knees to suddenly weaken and the Captain reached to support and lower her into a chair at the cabin table. The Captain expected her to completely break down into tears but instead Marianne looked him directly in the eye and asked, "Captain Boyle, with your permission I would like my husband to be buried at sea? His Grandfather was a Captain and I think it would be appropriate."

"As you wish, Mrs. Darcy. If it is any consolation I am honored to have known your husband even for this short time. He was a very brave man."

Marianne sat in the chair and as soon as the cabin door closed she covered her face with her hands and broke into tears. Here she was a new wife, a mother to be and a widow. Somehow she would manage when the ship arrived in America, her new home.

Chapter Two

Harmony Hill plantation was located in the foothills of the Appalachian Mountains in a very large fertile valley and not far from the Seven Hills of Rome. A river runs through the valley, between and around the endlessly rolling green hills. Cherokee Indians primarily populated the area.

Ashley always felt an overwhelming sense of deep pride as he rode through Harmony Hill plantation each morning on his rounds. The hills covered with hundreds of varieties of wild flowers surrounded the plantation. The long dusty road leading up to the ranch house was lined with multi colored Crepe Myrtle trees.

The wonderful and lucrative peach orchard was starting to flower and looked as though there would be a really good bumper crop this year. Along with the orchard there were several hundred acres cultivated for cotton, barley, peanuts, corn and many other vegetables. The cattle, horses and hogs had a thousand acres of free range to graze on which had many cold streams for water.

He had inherited this paradise from his Father as his Father did before him. Ashley's mother had been very ill for several years before she passed and his Father never quite recovered from her passing. Harmony had fallen into disrepair during that time when his father had languished over the death of his beloved wife.

Ashley wanted to marry Melanie soon after the first year of mourning but he had wanted to get the place back into a money making ranch and in first class order. They had known each other from the time they were both toddlers. Melanie was the only daughter of a neighboring plantation owner, not quite as large as Harmony. Harmony was a well established and profit making business for the family. Melanie, a true quintessential Southern Belle and of course was a spoiled Prima Donna. Ashley felt that perhaps she would not be up to the demanding tasks ahead of helping to run a large cattle ranch until he hired enough men.

At Melanie's insistence they married and he quickly found that he had been badly mistaken. Melanie fell right into the daily routine of rising early, often before daybreak, fixing breakfast for the two of them, gathering the eggs and feeding the chickens. She never complained even once about having blisters on her hands or about the dirt smudges on her beautiful angelic face. After a year of hard work and even with Melanie being with child the work of repairing the ranch was completed.

Thankfully Biddy, Melanie's nanny and nurse since her birth had came along with her. Biddy managed to keep her from over exertion and made her rest and eat properly. Even the blessings of pregnancy had problems but thankfully most were limited to sickness in the mornings. After Margie was born Biddy's job became two fold, that of caring for Melanie and Margie. Margie was twice as active and rambunctious as Melanie had ever been.

Ashley expanded Harmony to breeding Arabian horses, as he dearly loved their strength, speed, refinement and endurance. Strong bones gave them high spirit and alertness. Their sensitivity and willingness helped him to treat them with competence and respect. This endeavor had become a very lucrative enterprise and was admired by his associates and his neighbors.

Margaret or Margie as they called her was born six months after the restoration of the plantation to its original beauty. She was healthy and feisty and full of vim and vigor which both of her parents adored. Melanie was sitting on the back verandah making the guest list for the invitations they would send out for the huge BBQ and pig roast they intended to have to celebrate Margie's birth as well as the renovation of Harmony.

"Good morning, my beautiful butterfly! And how are you this bright and sunny day?" asked Ashley.

"Good morning my darling husband! I am just wonderful and busy writing up the guest list for the big event we are planning. I am so looking forward to meeting all of our neighbors and see some of my friends again. Do you think we will have the patio and BBQ pit finished by then as well as the gardens?"

"I don't think there will be a problem, the masons have been busy daily and will soon be finished with the project. Sweetheart, I think that I should start rounding up the cattle that we will be moving to Atlanta for sale before the festivities begin. It should not take too terribly long and will be one less thing to get done. I might also take some of the hogs as well since they have been fattened up nicely."

"That's a good idea Darling."

Melanie was still in the process of unpacking and placing some of the lovely antique gifts they received at their wedding reception. She wanted to find the perfect place to showcase them. As she gently unwrapped each one she marveled at them knowing that they would be perfect heirloom pieces to pass down through the family.

There had been so much to do this last year with Margie's birth and getting set into the running of the plantation house. She wished she could move along a bit faster and be a little more organized but with time she felt it would all fall into place. She wanted to get more involved with all the activities at the church and help out with the bake sales and the quilting projects that the ladies had going. All the profits from these projects went toward the less fortunate families and children who attended the church.

There were times when she felt that she was running in circles. She also worked in the church nursery during the Sunday services and loved being with all the babies and small children. Ashley was always after her to slow down some and not try to do so much but she felt she wasn't doing enough.

Ashley realized there was an awful lot of preparation to be done for the cattle and hog roundup. The stock pens still had to be prepared in order to separate the cows and calves from the steers as well as getting the brands checked to make sure that they didn't corral some of the neighbor's cattle. There were also some of the younger proven breeding cows and steers that they would keep as well as the calves. Also the proven hogs would be retained for future breeding. With hundreds of free pasture acres these herds could travel quite a distance especially if something spooked them.

Wylie Clegg was the head honcho and was getting the teams of riders together for the roundup. They would probably need at least thirty cowboys for the roundup as well as using some of them to prepare the pens. They would probably move 2,000 to 3,000 head and ten riders at any given time to keep watch on the herd. Each man would need three fresh horses to rotate if needed for each shift.

Thankfully they only had to move the heard seventy miles north as the crow flies to Atlanta's stockyards, which would take probably three and a half days barring any problems. It would take a couple of weeks to get the pens ready and no telling for sure how long to round up the cattle and the pigs. It shouldn't be too hard to locate the swine since they had a tendency to bunch together and loved the wooded areas the best. It was the cattle that would take the time through the whole process.

They had plenty of logs and lumber from the forest area around Harmony so that would be no problem. They would also have to take along a chuck wagon because the men had to have breakfast and lunch and supper each day of travel to Atlanta and on the way back. The trip back would be much quicker and they could make it in two or three days. Ashley wasn't concerned he had confidence in his foreman and crew and they would get the job done.

This would be the first time that Ashley would be away since he and Melanie married and he really didn't like leaving her. He knew she would be in good care with Biddy and Lydia the cook and her husband Able who was the houseman. There would still be a small crew left at the plantation including the gardener Clemmons. So he knew that Melanie and Margie would be in safe hands and he wouldn't be gone all that long but he still felt a little guilty leaving her so soon after the birth of Margie. Melanie would most likely stay busy with the baking sales and the quilting club as well as the church ladies and their teas. He was very proud of his wife and he told her so every day.

The next morning Ashley checked over the patio and BBQ pit as well as the fountain and gazebo, which was a wish of Melanie's. They also had many covered picnic type tables. The project was completed and all was set for the event they were planning in a month or so. The garden surrounding the area was just beautiful with its rose rushes and evergreen bushes and trees. Crepe Myrtle's lined the driveway leading back to the area. There were also Magnolia trees and weeping willows down by a creek at the back of the area with a blanket of green grass for Margie to play with a swing that he had built on a low limb of one of the willows and a sand box and slide. He really enjoyed making this play area for her even though at this time she was a bit too small to appreciate it.

The work was progressing on the pens and the men were out starting to round up the hogs first since that would probably be the easiest thing to do since they most likely did not travel as far as the cattle would. A few of the men were getting all the tack ready they would need as well as making sure the chuck wagon was in good repair and stocked and ready to roll..

Old Wiggens would take care of the cooking for the crew the same as he did at the bunkhouse for the men. He was a wily old guy who was always singing and laughing and telling jokes. The men loved him and looked after him since he did like to take a nip for the old white lightening jug now and then. Ashley knew he would not go at all if he couldn't take Rubbish his old hound dog with him. The two were never far out of sight of each other. Rubbish didn't care much for the mother cat and her kittens that showed up at the plantation one day. Melanie thought they were adorable and adopted them. She named her Snowball since she was as white as snow. Ashley figured they would end up keeping the whole bunch since Margie also loved them and she knew how many there were even though she couldn't count yet.

Melanie still busy with her guest list and a list of the cakes she wanted to give to Lydia so she could have them ready to give to Ashley to pick up some of the fixings on his trip back home through Atlanta. They needed a lot of flour and cornmeal every day for the bread and cakes. Melanie wanted to go into town and see the ladies at the church and find out what they needed for the next bake sale and drop of some swatches for the quilts they were working on as well as to see Pastor McDaniel about getting Margie baptized. She would take the small buggy to town and take Biddy and Margie with her to show off to the ladies and to the Pastor. She would go in the morning tomorrow. There seemed to be no end to all the tasks that she had to do but she loved each and every moment of it and was happy to stay busy.

Ashley hitched up the horse and loaded the rear of the buggy with everything Melanie was taking to town. She was taking a crock of beans and some cornbread for the Pastor as well as the cloth swatches for the ladies and everything she needed to take for Margie. It was quite a load by the time she got through picking out everything. She would have to remember to also pick up some thread in town on her way to the church. She hadn't been in on the quilt making much lately with so very much to do at home but she hoped to get back to it soon and she missed chatting and passing the time and catching up on all the gossip in town.

The short trip to town was uneventful and time passed rather quickly on the way. The ladies were very happy to see her and Margie. They couldn't seem to take their hands off of the baby and of course Margie loved every minute of all the attention she was getting.

"I will be able to do the Baptism when ever you are ready my dear," said Pastor Daniel. "It will be my blessed pleasure. We want to make sure our little angel is protected from all the evils in this world."

"Thank you so much Pastor. I am so sorry we have not attended church on a regular basis lately," said Melanie in an apologetic manner, "but so much at the plantation requires our presence these days. I do miss it and so does Ashley. At the present time he is busy getting ready to roundup the cattle and hogs to take to Atlanta. It requires a great deal of preparation."

"I understand completely my dear," responded Pastor McDaniel, "and just know that you are always in our thoughts and prayers."

"Thank you so much Pastor we will see you very soon. I must go and collect Biddy and Margie and stop off at the general store to pick up several items needed at home." At the general store she told the man behind the counter what she needed and he quickly filled her shopping list.

As she waited inside the store Biddy came in through the front door carrying Margie in her arms. Melanie asked the counter man if he could please load her packages into the buggy and he said of course. Then she turned and said, " Come along Biddy we must get on our way back home. I want to be home to have lunch with Ashley and talk about the plans for the roundup and see how everything is progressing. I am sure that Margie is also hungry by now with all this excitement she will probably sleep all the way home."

As they pulled up in the wagon to the front of the plantation Ashley was just riding up. He dismounted and tied his horse to the hitching post and then he helped Melanie carry in the items that were purchased. "You look lovely my Darling after your outing! How did everything go?" he asked. "It was good to get out and see everyone," answered Melanie as she continued putting the goods away. "I spoke with Pastor McDaniel about baptizing Margie and he said that anytime we are ready to just let him know and that we are in their thoughts and prayers."

"How are all the preparations going Sweetheart?" she asked.

"We are moving right along, most of the repairs are done on the pens and the crew has some of the hogs in already. They will go out this afternoon for the rest of the hogs and begin tomorrow on the cattle. If they keep up at this pace we should be ready to leave the first of the week for Atlanta. Old Wiggins is so happy to be making the trip that he is all but jumping out of his boots for joy."

"Rubbish caught a couple rabbits this morning so Wiggins will be cooking them some time today. The old hound is a good hunter!"

"I believe I will fully enjoy having some rabbit stew for supper tonight."

Chapter Three

In her private moments Marianne grieved the loss of James, her husband and set about getting settled in her new home New Orleans. She was appalled at the rudeness of the people in their manner and means of doing business. It seemed their only concern was earning a living, which was understandable but their methods often left much to be desired. The landlord, with whom she made an arrangement for her lodging, was probably the worst of the lot. He knew she was a new arrival to America and charged an exorbitant amount for the purchase of a small house in a section of town just outside the slum areas around the French Quarter of New Orleans.

Captain Boyle had been very insistent she take a large portion of the spoil that was found in the cargo holds of the pirate ship. The amount was in excess of a half million dollars in gold and silver coin. The Captain himself and several of the crew escorted her to a local bank ashore where the money was deposited. He explained it was a small price for the bravery and courage her husband had exhibited while defending the Chasseur.

It took a short amount of time for the ship's crew to transfer her few belongings from the ship's cargo hold to the new house. She thanked them for their help and as the last man started to leave down the walkway to go back to the ship he turned, took his cap off and said, " Missy, I just want to say you are a strong woman and you hold your grief inside well and if you will forgive me for being so forward I know the child you are carrying will grow to be a strong and upright man. You will have but one Grandchild, a girl."

"How do you know of these things?" asked Marianne. "A mother often knows what her child will be but how do you know such information?" As she stood there at the end of the walkway leading to the house she looked at the man standing in front of her. He wore the usual colorful scarf tied around his head, a small brass ring in one ear, short knickers and slightly dirty shirt of a typical sailor but he had very strange dark eyes that spoke of mystery and intrigue.

"It is the nature of my people, Missy. We are called wanderers or gypsies if you prefer. I also tell you this, the son that you carry will not grow to be a man of great age." Marianne was puzzled at the man's message but thanked him and offered him a coin for the information but he declined so she wished him fortune on his journey through life. She watched as the strange man walked down the short paved path and turn as he carefully closed the gate behind him.

The idea of her being a widow in a strange country was daunting but to be with child and not having a father figure for the baby was a heavy enough burden for any woman. Her father had taught her to be independent and trust no strangers until they prove themselves to be honest and upright. With the gold and silver the Captain had so graciously given her she would start a new life for herself and her newborn son.

Time passed slowly for Marianne as she prepared for the arrival of her child. Clothing continued to be a problem. It seemed she constantly had to buy ever-larger dresses to accommodate the new life she was carrying. Walking the short distance to various stores to buy food and apparel was not a problem in the early stages of her pregnancy but she knew soon she would have to make some type of arrangements to buy both. A knock on her door provided an answer.

"Yes, can I help you?" she asked as she opened the door. In front of her stood a young boy of perhaps ten years of age.

"Yes, Mamn. If you have some errands to do I can do them for you. I have both a horse and wagon for big errands and if you need help around the house I can do that as well." Marianne was impressed with his manners and courtesy but was also a little cautious.

"A horse and wagon. Does the horse belong to your father?"

"No Mamn. He is mine. I bought him two years ago with money I earned myself. He is a little old but the smithy said there is still plenty of good years left. He lets me keep him at the stable and I work there on weekends cleaning out the stalls to pay for his feed and hay."

Marianne looked at the lad. His clothes were home spun and were probably made by his mother and she liked him right away. "If you can come by every morning before school I would need for you to go to the general store for me to buy food and cloth so I can sew dresses and things."

"That would be great Mamn but I don't go to school. I never learned to read."

"Young man, that is absolutely shameful. How do you expect to grow up and become a businessman?"

"Yes, Mamn but when Papa died two years ago I had to become the man of the house and take care of my mother and younger sister." She felt badly because she had been harsh with the young boy and judged him prematurely. "Do you have a name?" she asked.

"Yes Mamn, it's Joseph Goldsmith."

"What is your normal rate for doing errands Joseph?"

"Depends on the job, Mamn but it's usually a nickel."

"A nickel it is then and if it is agreeable with your mother I can teach you to read, write and do numbers. A good businessman has to know how to add and subtract if they are going to be successful."

"Yes Mamn! I'll be here first thing every morning!" The broad smile on Joseph's face told Marianne it would be a very good bargain. She wondered about the child she was carrying and if the gypsy was correct and it was a son what would he grow up to be? In the months that followed the arrangement with Joseph did indeed turn out to be a good one and she was amazed at how quickly he learned to read and write. Numbers came very easily for him and one day he presented her with a small ledger that he had made. As she looked at the rows of neatly written numbers she noticed two sets. One she recognized from errands he had done for her but the other set was much smaller.

"This is very good Joseph and the totals are correct. I am extremely proud of you. I notice two sets of numbers. Can I ask what they are for?"

"Well, Yes Mamn but it would have to be our secret."

"Fair enough and you have my word it will be our secret."

"One row is for regular stuff like I do for people like you and the townsfolk and the other row is money my mother makes for doing washing and sewing. It is hard work and I hope to make enough so she won't have to do the washing clothes any more."

Marianne's eyes misted as she looked at the boy-man standing on the walkway in front of her. A boy who, because of circumstances, had to grow up far too quickly and the years that he would have spent fishing and swimming would be used working to provide for his mother and sister. "Your mother must be very proud of you Joseph," she said as she hugged him in her arms.

The months went by quickly and Marianne regularly went to see the Doctor for checkups and he told her she should deliver within a month and he was correct. William James Darcy was born exactly three weeks later.

Lawrence E. Claibourne, like his father and Grandfather before him was a rich man. Not only did he own a large section of the land in the French Quarter of New Orleans but he had inherited several cotton mills from his Grandfather as well. He was accustomed to having bankers and merchantmen seeking his advice on financial matters and even the mayor had asked on several occasions if he wanted to run for town councilman. He said no to the offer and gave the reason he was an honest businessman and not a politician. At thirty years old he was already a millionaire.

Even though he was rich he knew the value of hard work and he had little time for the finer side of society such as concerts and balls. His mother had taken him with her to many operas; in spite of adamant objections from his father so he knew of fine wine and dancing but felt it was a waste of good time and chose to pursue business ventures instead. There was strong talk of war every day and he felt in a time of war money could be made. One morning while sitting at his desk he opened the morning mail and found an invitation to attend a festival celebrating the anniversary of the town's founding. He accepted the invitation even though he felt it would probably be filled with over dressed people who drank too much.

Just on a whim he decided to go in costume even though Fat Tuesday or Mardi Gras wasn't supposed to officially start for another three days. On one other Mardi Gras celebration he had attended on casual observation he noticed every one seemed to either go as a red devil with forked tail and trident or Cinderella with her flowing silk and lace brocade gown. He decided that his costume would be that of a pirate. Of course his shirt would be clean and white with ruffles at the sleeve and throat. For added effect he selected a heavy highwayman's pistol, which he stuck in his front belt and a fine lightweight dueling saber rode in its scabbard at his waist. A very colorful scarf tied around his head, short knickers and heavy buckled shoes completed his costume. He looked at himself in a full-length mirror in the hallway of his house before he went out the door and smiled.

Instead of driving himself to the ball in a buggy he hailed a carriage as he was standing at the curb in front of his house. The carriage driver gave him a look over twice as he stepped down to open the side door for him and then asked, " Getting an early start on the festivities I see, Mr. Claibourne. No mask Sir?

"No, I decided to not wear one. I had thought of perhaps a patch over one eye to add to the effect but decided that might be a little too much."

"You are quite right, Sir. The pistol and sword are a very good touch."

"Thank you. Shall we go?"

On the way to the ball he rode in silence and watched as they passed other couples in costume on the walkway. Their conversation was hurried and excited but they seemed to be in no hurry and walked slowly, arm in arm. He had no time for marriage now perhaps in five or ten years after he had the business well established and making money. It was a fairly short ride and he paid the driver as he opened the small side door and stepped down.

He stood there on the street for several minutes and watched as people went up to the large wooden door, knocked and were let in by a well-dressed butler. Soft music filtered out onto the street in the brief moment the door was opened. *Do I really want to do this?* He asked himself. *The evening will undoubtedly be a total bore filled with people who drink too much and talk too loudly. Well, better to get it over with now that I am here.*

Lawrence went up to the door and knocked lightly. It was immediately opened by the butler who asked," Your invitation, Sir?" From his small waist pocket he produced his invitation and handed it to the butler. "Yes, Mr. Claibourne." The butler bowed from the waist as he stepped slightly backward to allow him to pass into the ballroom.

Lawrence was right and chuckled as he looked around at some of the guests. Most were dressed gallantly and some were, like him in costume but not all as he had presumed as devils and Cinderella. It seemed fantasy was in style that night. There were many ladies dressed as angels in long white gossamer flowing gowns, a few impish pixies and there were even a few ballerinas in their pink and white silk ruffled tutus. There was one costume there that night he did not expect to see and that was another pirate, like himself except this was obviously a female pirate.

He watched as she walked among the guests and chatted with several of the prominent businessmen who appeared to know her quite well. He guessed she was a prostitute but then he wondered how she had managed to acquire an invitation to the ball? Perhaps one of her clientele had arranged the invitation he reasoned. He didn't trifle with ladies of the night as they usually carried dreadful diseases in spite of precautions. But still he couldn't help but watch as she walked and the way she carried herself with a sense of deep pride. It wasn't haughty like most ladies of society but more of self-assurance. He found himself standing just to one side of her as she finished a conversation with the mayor. She turned and it was like he was looking at a royal queen. He was at a loss for words.

"Yes, monsieur?" she asked. Her voice was that of an angel. " Parlez **vous** francais?"

"I am terribly sorry, miss or madam," he stammered, "I do not speak French although I understand it is a magnificent language."

"Yes," she responded in English, " and it rolls so smoothly off the tongue. I do prefer English actually."

"Thank you. I could not help but notice we have the same costume tonight. I was expecting devils in red with forked tails and Cinderella's."

"I too was expecting the traditional costumes and decided to be different. To be absolutely truthful I had not wanted to attend but found myself accepting the invitation. Since my husband died a year ago I have become a recluse and tonight is a refreshing change."

"If I may be so forward Mrs…?"

"Darcy, James Darcy."

" Mrs. Darcy, I believe the band is playing a waltz and my name is Lawrence Claibourne. May I have the honor?"

"You may indeed, Mr. Claibourne."

That night of dancing led to a whirlwind romance filled with travel to exotic places in the orient and middle east and one evening over a luscious dinner Lawrence asked as he presented her with a ring, "Marianne I know it has been only three months but would you marry me? If it is agreeable a formal adoption for William can be legalized. As a general rule I prefer the universities in Europe simply because it is a much better education and I will be more than happy to arrange it for him."

"What can I say except yes and yes."

Chapter Four

Willliam felt a little intimidated while walking around the Oxford University grounds with Lawrence Claibourne his stepfather. The buildings were so big and there were so many people hurriedly going about their business of getting an education.

"In a few years William this is where you will be going, "said Lawrence as he waved his arm toward the red and brown brick buildings. "I have talked with the headmaster and your tuition has already been paid for a full six years plus you will be staying in the dormitories provided by the school. Food and a monthly allotment to spend has all been arranged. Before you start your education here however, you will be staying at a private boarding school. A gentleman has to have a good education if they are going to be a success in the world today."

The trip across the Atlantic a week earlier had been a unique experience for William. He had never been aboard a ship before and just standing in the bow with the wind and an occasional spray of salty seawater blowing in his face was very exciting. He was just big enough to look over the wooden bulwark of the ship's railing and watch as the ocean went by in smooth rolling waves. He was amazed as the deck hands scurried about doing their chores and keeping the ship seaworthy. High overhead in the crow's nest a sailor looked through a long metal glass watching for other ships. Mostly the sailors smoked pipes and cursed a lot as they worked.

Mr. Claibourne had adopted him three years before or so his mother had told him anyway. They lived in New Orleans and he could speak a few French words and he even knew a few cuss words in French but his mother scolded him harshly whenever he said them. "William James Claibourne I will wash you mouth out with soap if you say those words again." Anytime she said his full name he knew he was in deep trouble.

New Orleans had just come through a major battle between the British and General Andrew Jackson. The British with 8,000 well-trained soldiers outnumbered Jackson's combined army with approximately 4,500 men. Jackson's army consisted of Creoles, blacks, businessmen, shoemakers and about five hundred "dirty shirts" from Kentucky. Should Jackson lose he would have lost New Orleans. If it had not been for the help and intervention of Jean Lafitte the privateer who provided men, gunpowder and musket flints at a crucial time America would have probably been lost as well. All William knew of the battle were stories the local people told about a lot of confusion, people running around the city and the air smelling of burned gunpowder.

His mother had chosen to stay behind in New Orleans instead of coming with them to England. She assured him she would write every week and he promised he would talk with the headmaster and get him to write letters to send back to her. He tried not to cry when his stepfather left him with the headmaster at the boarding school. "It is better this way William," he assured him, "An education is vital and I am confident in the few years ahead you will grow into manhood. You mother and I will anxiously await your return to America after completion of studies at Oxford." He watched as his stepfather and the headmaster shook hands then closed the door behind him as he left the headmaster's office. He was alone for the first time in his life.

In the many months that followed that meeting between his stepfather and the headmaster he learned the harsh and sometimes-painful reality of life and discipline in a boarding school. It seemed he was punished almost daily for some infraction of the school's guidelines or rules. Most of the other students were slightly older than he and had been at the school for a lot longer. They constantly played practical jokes and pranks on the faculty and were punished accordingly. He never participated in any of their antics but he was often punished for being in the wrong place at the wrong time. The punishments were always limited to a few well-placed strokes of a thick oak board to his buttocks. One day the headmaster called him into his office

"Mr. Claibourne I am disappointed in your participation in some of the activities partaken of by your fellow students. I had thought you enjoyed your stay better than to involve yourself with that type of things."

"I do enjoy staying here, Sir," responded William. "My stepfather impressed upon me the value of a good education."

"Then why do you participate in practical jokes like your fellow students? All this does is cause disruptions."

"No Sir, I don't participate," argued William, " They are my friends and I just like to be with them."

"Mr. Claibourne you mean to say you just stand around and watch?"

"Yes, Sir, Headmaster. I see no value in embarrassing someone with nonsense but I do enjoy being with my friends. I have so very few. One of them is good with mathematics; another is good with managing money, while another is good with history and government."

"Do you not think we have good education facilities here, Mr. Claibourne?"

"Yes, Sir but it seems lacking at times and I want more so I ask my friends many questions, when they aren't fooling around of course."

"Young William I have underestimated you and I apologize. You have wisdom far beyond your ten years of age and I am sure you will do well in life. Your stepfather has arranged things for you to continue here until you are thirteen and then on to Oxford for four years."

"Thank you Headmaster. My stepfather means well and he provides well for my mother and I. My mother told me a few things of my real father, James Darcy about how he died aboard the Chasseur going to America."

"James Darcy was your father?" asked the headmaster as he leaned forward across the huge wooden desk in front of him.

"Yes, Sir, James R. Darcy."

"Well, that explains it then. Your father was a student here and he was just as earnest and curious of new things and learning about them. When he left our school at thirteen years of age he was at the top of his class. I did hear of him, as he grew older however. He had quite a reputation with the ladies and a bit of a scoundrel. Your mother must have been quite a lady to have tamed him. All that aside young William you come from excellent stock. You may return to your classes."

The next two years passed quickly for William. After the meeting with the Headmaster he severely limited his activities of playing pranks with his friends. He used the excuse of being behind in his studies when they would ask him to join them and they chided him for being a bore and would often leave him behind and laughed as they walked away. One fellow however did not always walk away but stayed behind.

"Are you not going with the others?" William asked.

"No, I think I would rather stay behind and chat if that is fine with you?" answered Nathan.

"Thank you and yes I would enjoy your company and chat."

"I am pleased, thank you. I used to enjoy that type of thing but as I have aged somewhat it is no longer fun. What would you like to talk about? I hate talking about other people. My father once said, " Only small people talk of other people behind their backs."

"I agree with your father so how about history or science?"

"Excellent suggestion. We ask each other ten questions and the one who correctly answers the most wins?"

"I like that," answered William, " But what would be the prize? We have to have a prize."

"A schilling is too much. How does five pence sound?"

"Five pence it is then," agreed William.

The afternoon passed quickly and the score was tied at eight questions each. It was William's turn to ask a question when a faculty member came running across the grass and stopped where the two of them were seated on benches across from each other at a stone table.

"Mr. Claibourne the Headmaster would like to speak with you in his office, immediately."

"Well we can't keep the Headmaster waiting, can we? Just remember it is my turn," William added as he looked across the table at his friend. As he seated himself in front of the large wooden desk he looked at the Headmaster and he was not smiling.

"Mr. Claibourne I have arranged passage on the next ship going to America to dock at New Orleans." The ominous tone of his voice told William he was about to hear very bad news. When his mother had told him about his father's death and how he had died he had shed not one tear. When the Headmaster told him his stepfather and Mother had passed away from yellow fever in New Orleans and he had just received a letter from Mr. Claibourne's business partner. His step father's partnership would be kept in escrow until he decided what to do with it. William just sat there at first then got up and walked over to a window and looked out at the trees across the grass. It was late summer and the trees were just beginning to change into their panorama of orange, gold and yellow. He turned and looked the Headmaster in the eye.

"Thank you Sir. I shall leave immediately and return quickly to finish here."

"That won't be necessary William. Next year is your final year and your grades are exemplary and like your father you are at the top of your class. I shall write a letter of commendation for you to take with you when you decide to continue your education at Oxford, if that is your wish?"

"It is and thank you again, Sir."

During the trip back over the Atlantic to New Orleans William kept to himself and only once went topside to stand at the ship's rail. The sea was very rough and a storm was in the air. Most of the ship's larger sails had been taken down in preparation to meet the storm and as he looked up at the crow's nest a gust of wind blew a mist of seawater into his eyes to mix with his tears. He had not cried either at the news of his father's death or his mother's but now the feelings he had kept hidden deep within rose up in his throat and he cried. Deep sobs racked his body as a seaman walked up to him.

"Are you okay?" he asked.

" Yes, thank you. Just some sea water got in my eyes."

"You should return to your cabin. It feels like she is going to blow tonight. A bad storm is in the wind," said the sailor as he looked up into the dark clouds that rolled across the sky.

"Thank you. Just a few minutes more."

The few minutes more turned into almost a full hour as William stood at the rail. The sailor had been correct and the storm's fierce winds howled through the ship's rigging causing the tall wooden masts to creak and grown in protest. Jagged lightning flashed across the dark clouds and was quickly followed by thunder that rolled across the sky like giant boulders. William's clothes were soaked and hung on him like wash fresh from the tub but he didn't care. He was angry that he was alone in the world and he was angry that both his mother and father had been taken away from him far too early. As his salty tears mixed with the salt of the waves that thundered over the ship's bow he looked up into the sky and asked, "Why?" He vowed that night to carefully guard his feelings, no matter the reason.

His stepfather's business partner was true to his word and arranged everything for the funeral services. Afterwards in his office he explained about the extensive business dealings of Mr. Claibourne's company. There were cotton plantations in Louisiana and Alabama along with mills to process the cotton into huge rolls of material and other plants to manufacture the cloth into clothes for the open market. As Mr. Claibourne had no other living relatives young William stood to inherit the complete business holdings of the company. Mr. Ruben offered to buy his share of the company but William declined.

"Mr. Ruben I greatly appreciate your generous offer but it is my intention to go back to England and complete my education then return to America and run the company with yourself as a partner. Would this be agreeable with you, Sir?"

"Yes and thank you. With your permission I would like to hire an overseer to run the cotton plants and mills here in Louisiana and explore the possibilities of expansion into Tennessee? Of course regular accountings would be forwarded to you in England."

"An excellent plan Mr. Ruben."

William at twelve years old was already very rich. During the return trip across the Atlantic the weather was extraordinarily beautiful for that time of year and he spent almost every waking hour topside chatting with the crew and several times he joined them as they worked with repairing the thick hemp ropes used for the ship's rigging.

The tools used for most rope repairs consisted of a very sharp knife, a steel marlinspike for small ropes and a wooden fid for large ropes. The sailors enjoyed his company and quickness to learn. In a short time they taught him the four common splices, back, eye, short and long. His favorite was the sail maker's splice where a loop was made at the end of a rope, which could be used for hanging things on a ship's bulkhead or a barn wall. William saw one of the sailors doing something with a small piece of hemp line. When he finished it didn't look like a splice and William asked what it was.

"This my lad" said the sailor as he held up the rope he had been working on, "Is the King Of Knots the bowline. In foul weather you want to depend on this knot to keep you from falling overboard should you have the unfortunate task of keeping watch in the crows nest." William asked if the sailor could teach him the knot and he watched as the deck hand slowly fashioned the knot. Then it was his turn and as he finished the deck hand slapped him on the back and said, "Well done lad. I do not know what fortune may lie at the end of your journey in England but you have quickness about you and an eagerness to learn. You would do well aboard a ship."

"Thank you and I admit I feel at home when the waves wash over the bow, the smell of salt in the air and it would be a grand life but my fortune it seems is already set for me. Perhaps later as I get a little older."

The opportunity to explore a life at sea never came for William. He returned to England and four years later he graduated from Oxford University with honors. Once again he found himself aboard a ship going to America. His stepfather's business in the cotton industry had blossomed and expanded. William's business partner had kept his word and after a lengthy and time-consuming arrangement expanded the company into Tennessee. William was seventeen.

Chapter Five

Ashley always had the greatest respect for the Cherokee Indian and many times he knew when hunting was not good that they would take a steer or two. He didn't mind because they were not greedy and the steer would be divided among the entire village. The pelts for rugs or blankets and the intestines would be used for fishing bait or trapping other wild animals. One way or other they didn't waste anything that God or nature provided. The squaws often times brought him and Melanie moccasins or beaded shawls and other woven goods. Melanie in turn when she baked bread would always make extra to take to them and she would make extra cookies for the Indian children. Sometimes the braves would also bring fish they had caught in the river. Melanie loved the little Indian children and often worked with them teaching them to learn to read and often gave them books. One couldn't possibly ask for a better relationship than Ashley and Melanie had with the Cherokee.

Every now and then the young braves trying to show their machismo would race the horses that Ashley had in the pastures. They never abused any of the animals so it was fine with him as they rubbed them down afterward and treated the animals with great respect and giving the horses extra exercise was always a benefit to the animal.

The Indians seemed to find great pleasure in helping his men with the roundup especially the young braves. There really wasn't a whole lot for them to do at their own camps so helping Ashley and the men after they had gotten their own hunting and fishing done was something they welcomed.

The roundup had gone well and all the cattle were in pens according to which were to be kept and which were to be sent to the cattle sale in Atlanta. The cows and calves were always prized and the best and largest of the steers were always kept for breeding purposes.

The roundup would not be complete without the help of the two Maremma sheepdogs that Ashley had acquired through a friend of his who brought them back from Italy over a year ago. The dogs very much resembled the Pyrenean Mountain Dog, the Kuvasz of Hungary, and the Akbash Dog of Turkey. Rebel and Rondo were a great asset with the herding of the cattle going to Atlanta and they were wonderful household pets that both Ashley and Melanie loved. They both were large dogs weighing close to a hundred pounds and stood about twenty-eight inches high. They have a long, harsh and very abundant coat that has a slight wave and a dense undercoat. They are very calm in the house since they have plenty of room to stretch their legs and get all the exercise they need. They also got along well with Rubbish, old Wiggins dog and Snowball the adopted mother cat and her kittens. Often times Margie fell asleep on the floor for her nap all curled up with all three of the dogs, her arms around Rubbish's neck.

They were just about ready to move them out on the next day when a huge storm front hit and knocked down a lot of the fences between the pens. There was some damage to the large barn, which had to be repaired before anything else was done. One of the outside fences had been broken in the storm and a few steers had got out so they would have to be found and brought back.

A few of the hogs were missing so they had to hunt them down as well. Hogs generally had a habit of rooting around for fresh tender roots and usually headed for the wooded areas. The steers on the other hand could be just about anywhere. Ashley was beginning to wonder if this roundup would ever get under way. It seemed as though one thing after another kept happening to slow things down but finally after three days they again had everything all sorted out. Now if everything went according to plan they would leave out a little before dawn the next day.

The chuck wagon was stocked and ready to go thanks to Old Wiggins and Wylie Clegg the cook had all the tack and gear ready. At sundown some of the men sat around the cook fire and sang songs. Someone had a guitar and another produced a banjo from somewhere. Most of the time cowboy songs consisted of a girl they left behind somewhere, a trail they had once been down or a town they had been in. It was sort of a way to celebrate the beginning of the drive because there was always the element of danger and hardship somewhere down the trail. After a few songs the men turned in early to be bright and full of vim and vigor for the start in the morning.

They started out bright and early the next morning with Ashley in the lead and the chuck wagon bringing up the rear. It was a nice sunny but cool day so hopefully things should go along without any problems. The night watch would have to be very careful since several ranchers had said they saw black panthers as well as cougars up among the rocks. Georgia is known for cougars and black panthers as well as bears and coyotes. The dogs liked to sometimes sleep out away from the camp among the herd so they would certainly let us know if anything is around and stalking the cattle.

It had been an uneventful day and after moving approximately fifteen miles they decided to camp for the night and get a start again at sunrise the next morning. Ashley had some difficulty getting to sleep thinking about Melanie and Margie back home and wishing he were there instead of on the hard ground looking up at the clear starlit sky. Morning would come long before any of the tired men were ready for it.

On the second day Ashley was up early and anxious to get a start on the day's drive hoping they might make a few more miles than they had the day before. Everything so far was moving along nicely. They had a whopping good breakfast of eggs, salt pork and several cups of good hot black coffee and Old Wiggins had put out a jar of honey that made the biscuits taste even better. Wiggins was a second-generation trail cook and his reputation was known throughout the ranches of Georgia.

Some green trail hand once asked Wiggins how he knew when the coffee was done. He looked the young cowboy in the eye and as he dried his hands on his leather apron said, "Well son it's like this. First you get a three pound size coffee can and fill it about three quarters full with barrel water or spring water if you can find it, then you put in a good handful of Arbuckle's coffee. Throw in a smidgen of salt for taste. Next you put 'er on the fire and let it come to a boil."

"I got that part," said the rookie," But how do you know when it's done?"

"That's the tricky part. The only way to know for sure is to find a horseshoe and toss it in. If it floats the coffee is done," answered Wiggins very seriously. By that time some of the older trail hands had gathered to listen as Wiggins talked and they all broke out laughing. The youngster realized he had been the butt of a joke and his face reddened in embarrassment.

The trail hands tried constantly to get Wiggins to tell them his white gravy recipe but he steadfastly refused using the reason it was one his Grandmother had passed down. Even if there wasn't time to sit and eat, two of his thick biscuits with sausage or bacon filled their belly. The night patrol had heard a coyote off in a distance but it stayed far away. The dogs seemed to be restless and were on the prowl almost all night.

Ashley's hip was bothering him where he had fallen over some rocks while out in the pasture the last week and he hoped it wouldn't continue to give him problems. There wouldn't be any doctor out here on the trail so he had no choice but to persevere. He would put a hot poultice on it when he retired for the night and hopefully by morning it would not hurt quite so much. He wished he were at home so that Melanie could put some liniment on it and hot compresses to stop the swelling. He wasn't usually so clumsy but that day he had something else on his mind and wasn't paying attention to where he was walking. He had a tendency now and then to daydream and go off in another place thinking of all the things he wanted to do and accomplish in the future.

Some of the men went out looking for the coyote before going to sleep because it's mournful howl seemed much closer and they didn't want it to spook the cattle. Ashley hoped it was only a coyote and nothing with two legs instead of four. After about an hour a distant single shot echoed through the darkness. One of the men had found and shot the coyote and after that the cattle seemed to quite down. They had made twenty miles today and everyone was totally worn out and ready for a nights sleep.

With any luck they would be able to make another eighteen or twenty miles tomorrow and that would only leave about fifteen or so miles for the next day. He was anxious to get back home. He knew there no reason to worry about Melanie and Margie because they were well looked after and he knew she would not venture far from the plantation with him away except into town for supplies. After another huge breakfast of eggs and bacon, biscuits and thick gravy and hot coffee they were again on their way toward Atlanta.

Sometime during the day Rebel and Rondo had found themselves a girlfriend. He couldn't tell what breed she was but she was all black and just about as large as they are. He supposed it would pose no problem there was plenty of room to add another dog to the growing group of dogs and cats at the plantation. He did hope they wouldn't get into a fight over her but at the moment they seemed quite content to share.

Ashley discovered that a mile or so behind them some of the young Indian braves were following them. He didn't think it was a problem they just wanted a little outing and were most likely just curious about where they were going and what they were doing. He decided to invite them to join the group for supper that night. He would rather they be with the group that were following behind.

The Indians were glad to join and also were very happy to have something to eat. They had been hunting rabbits or whatever they could find on the way. After a large meal they all settled down without any hesitation to go to sleep again completely worn out from the riding and herding all day. Early the next morning long before sunrise Ashley heard a rustle of clothing. He turned slowly on his hard bed on the ground to watch as the young braves untied their unshod ponies at the picket line and walk away into the gray dawn.

It was almost morning anyway so he rolled out from underneath the blanket, picked up his saddle that had been his pillow for the night, walked to his horse and slung the saddle across the bay mare's back. As he finished tying everything down he heard a noise behind him and quickly turned around to see Old Wiggins coming out from behind some sagebrush.

"Getting the morning's business done Wiggins?" he asked. "Just the usual stomach trouble boss from too much coffee late at night," answered Wiggins. "Breakfast is ready if you want to roust out the hands?" "Sounds good. We need to have a good day today so it won't be a long one tomorrow into Atlanta." "Gotcha boss. Say, don't tell the hands but I keep some Kentucky special recipe underneath the wagon seat to sweeten up your coffee. I know you have a rule against liquor on the trail but it might help your hip a little." "Thanks, I'll keep it in mind, just in case."

Chapter Six

At Dirty Harry's Saloon outside Atlanta a local group of rustlers were talking about how they missed out on stealing some of the steers last week when that drive came through. Pardy Wilcox was arguing over their not being able to get a decent plan together. "What the hell is wrong with you guys? Have you all lost your nerve?" he asked. Bobo Ransom replied as he spat a wad of black chewing tobacco juice onto the ground, "Nope, you didn't come up with a decent enough plan Pardy. It's a big job and we couldn't go in with your half-baked ideas." "We need all the men with this and most of you couldn't make up your minds whether you were in or out," Pardy argued back. Cal Prosper slammed his fist on the table and knocked over several glasses of whiskey in the process. "Who the hell is running this outfit anyway?" he bellowed.

Pardy replied, "With everybody Ruff, Mort and Turpo, that makes six of us and that should be enough to do the job. There is a drive coming in from Harmony. They won't be expecting anything to happen this close to town and should be easy pickings. "From Harmony?" one of the men asked. "There will be at least a dozen riders not counting that hard case Ashley. He may have a funny sounding name but he is plenty mean when you get down to it. How does that figure into your plan?"

"You against killing a few men if the pay is worth it?" answered Pardy.

"Well, if you put it that way not at all," said the cattle thief as he drained his glass of whiskey.

Pardy was the brains of the rowdies, the men all trusted him and he had earned their respect by never putting them down in front of the others. He realized they had to figure out where to move the herd so they could change the brand before moving them to market. Ashley was a big cattle rancher but he did not brand every animal in his herd and that made it a whole lot easier.

According to Pardy's new plan Mort's ranch was the furthest and in a Southerly direction since they were not going to sell the cattle in Atlanta but in Auburn which was much closer. There another group of men would move them in the direction of Columbus, Georgia where there were military bases close by and they would be easy to sell to the government. The sooner the cattle were out of their hands the better.

Pardy reasoned after they took care of Ashley and the drivers they would start out with as many as they could get the first time and hold them at Mort's until the next night when they got some more. If they could get as many as a hundred head or more to the Auburn stockyards every night it wouldn't take to long.

Ashley had about 4000 head so hopefully they would be grouped together and a small roundup would be easier. With the plan set for tomorrow a little before sunrise they had a couple more beers and took off for home to meet back at Dirty Harry's early in the evening the next night.

What the rustlers didn't know was the bartender and owner of Dirty Harry's had overheard their plans and went to see Ashley as soon as he closed up. It would be pretty late so he decided to leave Woody his partner to close and that way he could leave out earlier. To him Ashley and his wife were really good people and he didn't want to see anything like this to happen to them. Melanie and his wife were good friends and worked a lot together at the church and with the children in the town and at school. They were both very hard working people and genuinely loved by all the people they associated with and who knew them.

All the ranch hands and owners knew about Dirty Harry's saloon. At any given time the tables and floor were covered with a fine layer of dust carried in with the hot wind. But Harry kept the bar and glasses clean so he knew the men used the term Dirty Harry's loosely and with affection.

It was only a couple miles to Harmony from the saloon and Harry hoped that he didn't have to wake everyone up as it was already past nine o'clock. As he rode up to the plantation all the lights except on the porch were out. He walked up to the door and pounded as loud as he could and then all the dogs started barking. Soon a light came on in the house and Margie came to the door. "So sorry to wake you up so late Mamn but I have some information for your husband that I picked up in the bar tonight." He spelled out the plan or what he heard of it. Margie thanked him and said Ashley had already started the trail drive to Atlanta. "Thank you Mamn. I know the direction they're headed and I'll try and catch them. My apologies for waking you up."

Harry then went to the rail where his horse was tied and with a spur to the mares flank he galloped off into the night. It was dangerous business riding after dark so he let the mare have her head and let her run trusting she could see in the dark a lot better than he could. After about a few hours hard ride he smelled smoke and knew he had found their camp. At the edge of the campsite he called out, " Hello the camp!" Someone yelled back, "Come on in if you're friendly!" He dismounted and tied his horse at the picket line then explained to Ashley what he had heard from the cattle thieves. They sat at the fire's edge and warmed themselves against the night's chill. "Is that coffee I smell?" asked Harry.

"Sure is," answered Ashley, "Wiggins made it for the night riders just before he turned in."

The two of them sat in silence after Harry had filled him in on the details he had heard the rustlers making. "Damn, I had hoped this would be an easy time of it but guess not, said Ashley"

"When I get back to town I'll wake up the sheriff, suggested Harry"

"Thanks I appreciate it."

"Tell Wiggins he makes a damn good cup of coffee."

"I will and you take care. Never know when your horse might find a gopher hole."

Ashley was feeling pretty bad about the pack of rustlers that would attempt to steal his herd. He knew that it had happened in the past to others but somehow he never thought he would be the next one targeted. No point in waking the men up now he would let them in on what was going to happen at breakfast in the morning. Ashley would go into town and let the sheriff in on what was supposed to happen. Then he would get together with the men and set their trap for the rustlers. The dogs would be their greatest warning in this little trap since they would let everyone know if anyone was out around the herd. He really hoped they could catch the whole group and put them in jail where they belonged before they could do anymore damage to anyone else.

Long before dawn Ashley got up and after a couple cups of strong, hot, black coffee went out to check and see where most of the herd was located so they would know where to lay their trap. Luckily there were many wooded areas and brush around so they could hide and wait. He figured it would be shortly after sunrise when they would hit and the dogs would be the early warning system.

The sheriff had twenty men with him. With Ashley's crew they would surely outnumber the cattle thieves. It wasn't quite sun-up yet as they waited in the thick underbrush and trees. They were well hidden and there would be no smoking, talking or moving around. It was a longer wait than they had expected. The sun was just coming up and everyone was getting anxious but then the dogs started barking and alerted everyone.

Pardy and Calhoun took off racing away from the herd in their attempt to get away. Wylie Clegg and Ashley were close behind and headed to cut them off. One shot rang out and Calhoun, wounded badly fell off his horse into the dirt. Pardy pulled up his horse, got off and waited to be caught. There was another shot in the distance and this time it was Mort who was shot. It took no time at all to have the six men rounded up and the herd quieted.

If all went well they would be having supper tonight in Atlanta, the herd all corralled and sold and be ready to return back to the plantation the next morning. Ashley wasn't at all sorry this roundup was at an end. He wanted to get back home to the warmth of his home and family. This was the first time he had been away from Melanie and of course Margie and he was really homesick for them. But as providence would have it Mother Nature had a surprise for them. Probably the one word that strikes fear in any cowhand is stampede.

The oldest member of the drive was Charlie Woodard. No one knew exactly how old he was and of course Charlie wasn't telling. To look at his face he looked as old as Methuselah. He had deep creases in his weather worn face but his deep blue eyes were clear underneath shaggy brows. He was probably a third generation cowhand and if anyone wanted to know anything about ranching or cattle Charlie was the man to go see.

He had the last half of the night watch and as he sat on his horse a familiar scent came riding in with the cool morning breeze, rain was coming. He quickly looked around where he was and didn't see any arroyos or deep gullies to watch out for in case of flash flooding so he just pulled up the collar on his sheepskin lined coat against the chill and sat stoically on his horse watching the horizon off to the east. Color was just beginning to show but he knew it was false dawn and too early for morning. As he watched the sky the stars to the west quickly disappeared one by one, the wind picked up and changed to a dry hot breeze. It meant trouble and it was coming their way. He spurred his horse to a gallop and rode into camp.

At the camp he kicked Ashley's boots and yelled, "Storms coming!" The hands quickly threw off their blankets and scrambled to put on their boots and chaps. Wiggins had already been up an hour preparing breakfast but no one stopped to grab a hot biscuit or even a cup of steaming black coffee on their way to mount their horses and get out to the herd. It was an eerie sight as they slowly rode around the edge of the cattle herd. The air was hot and sticky and in the early morning darkness St. Elmo's fire danced and jumped from the cattle's horns. Suddenly a bolt of hot, white lightning struck a tree off in the distance and the boom that followed was all that was needed to spook the herd!

Immediately everyone tried to keep the herd together by yelling and some even shot their pistol in the air but it was no use, as a single unit the cattle broke into a stampede. Ashley yelled above the din of thundering hooves, "Let them run!" He saw the direction they were running and it was the way towards Atlanta. A stampede is dangerous business but if the cattle wanted to go that direction in a hurry it would save a lot of time so all they had to do was make sure the herd wasn't running towards any gullies or rivers up ahead. Wiggins would catch up when he could.

Amazingly the entire herd arrived at the stockyard in Atlanta, except one newborn calf that got separated from its mother during the storm. At the stockyards Ashley sat on his horse with the lost calf across his saddle and watched as a man moved his hand back and forth to count the cattle as they moved through the chute into the holding pens. That night the sounds of men celebrating a successful drive lasted well into the early hours of morning.

Chapter Seven

As time passed Atlanta grew and prospered and along with it the plantations, ranches and farms. The merchants were thriving and the population was growing. Harmony also expanded and Ashley and Melanie's family also grew. Melanie had two miscarriages during a five-year period and two years later the twins Adam and Jacob were born. Ashley was in seventh heaven now with two boys to pass his legacy on to and teach them everything he knew so that when the time came they would be ready to take over the ranch. The twins now twelve years old managed to get into every kind of trouble they could find once their chores were done and they had free time.

Margaret now a month away from her seventeenth birthday had been well tutored through the years by her Mother and was in turn teaching the younger children in the small church in town. She loved working with the children and her patience was endless. She also was part of the church choir.

Margaret and her Mother were also making plans for a big party for her birthday a month away. She was a very popular girl courted by many of the young men and attended many parties and gatherings with the teens of her age. They hoped to make this a sort of coming out party for her as well and introduce her to some of the society of Atlanta.

Ashley fitted out a small cart for Margaret to ride back and forth to town in with a gentle well-mannered mare to pull it. Both of them still baked for the bake sales and occasionally took some fresh baked goods with them when they visited the sick and elderly

Adam and Jacob were also a responsibility that Margaret took on from the time they were babies and keeping up with them was no easy task. They had a habit much to everyone's dismay of wandering off with out anyone's permission or knowledge. They were extremely adventurous and the Spook Owl Mountains off in the distance a mile or two away called to them and peaked their curiosity. The mountains were so named because the people who lived closer to them heard the owls at night. The hills and valleys were very dark because of the heavy forestry that seemed to stretch up to the sky. Sometimes early in the morning you could watch as the clouds seemed to come and kiss the tops of the trees. Even if you only went a little ways into the deep woods it was hard to see the sky through the treetops.

Adam and Jacob were trying to hatch a plan with a couple of the Indian boys to go to the mountains and into the woods to see what they could discover. They had heard some of the men talking about gold being found and colored stones that were called quartz and beryl as well as amber that had little tiny bugs and things trapped in the stones and are all supposed to be valuable. Some of the stones were clear and gold colored like the sun and some were purple, the beryl stones were red and clear and some red ones that you could not see through and these were very hard to find.

The boys knew they would have to pick a time when their Mother and Father were off in town or on a chore and only Margaret would be home but she was usually busy with baking or teaching and not watching them all the time. Biddy would be busy in the house with the cleaning and both Old Wiggins and Wylie Clegg would be busy with the heard.

Adam was the ringleader and decided they should leave out early in the morning. He outlined his plan and told each brave what his duties would be before they could leave. "Jacob you be responsible for getting us some sour dough bread, hardtack biscuits and a jar of jam or sorghum molasses. I will get us some salt pork and a knife and skillet, some flint rock and fill the canteens with water. Motock and Bendbow will bring some blankets and some bows and arrows and extra knives. I am sure we will find some water there but just in case we have to take some extra canteens. Jacob see if you can find some pans out around the bunkhouses we could use to pan for the gold. I'm pretty sure I heard Mom telling Biddy they were going to town early and for her to shop and check in at the church and father had to go to the hardware for some tack and things for the horses and with all that going on should be gone for all morning and most of the day."

The boys didn't seem to mind Adam taking charge of their adventure. He just sort of had a knack for being the leader. "Oh! Lets not forget to take rope with us just in case we need it. We can make our backpacks from the blankets and roll everything inside that we need to carry, tying the canteens to our belts." Then as everyone was running around getting the stuff ready he yelled out, "Don't forget some fish hooks, there may be some streams or ponds in the woods where we can fish. We can hide the stuff in the back of the barn where all we have to do is pick it up and move out in the morning after Mom and Dad leave."

The next morning after their mother and father left and Biddy had fixed their breakfast they hurried out to the barn. Motock and Bendbow were waiting for them ready for their great adventure. "It's probably going to take us an hour or more to get to the bottom of the mountain," Jacob said.

By the time they reached the mountain the boys were already a bit tuckered out and had to sit and rest for a bit before starting to climb. It wasn't very steep at this point but just enough so they couldn't ride the horses. They were well below the tree line. It didn't take very long for the forest to surround them and it got darker as the sun almost directly overhead was blotted out. They could hear the sound of the birds chirping and calling to each other as other smaller animals ran through the brush. They weren't exactly sure what kind of critters were in these woods and their imaginations were running a bit wild. Adam whispered to Bendbow, " Do you think there are any bears in these woods?"

"I don't know about bears but I have heard some of the older braves talking about animals bigger than bears in here." Bigger than bears Adam wondered. What could be bigger than a full-grown bear?

After they walked for several hours they were already getting tired and decided to sit down and have a snack and rest awhile. Adam all of a sudden said, "You know what! We have no way of knowing what time it is because it is so dark in here. We will never know when it's night." Jacob replied, " We can keep looking up and hope to see a break in the trees and maybe see the stars or the moon. Anyway you think about it when we are so worn out we can't walk anymore then I suppose it will be night and we better start on the way back home. If we don't get home tonight Mom and Dad are going to be really mad and will have a whole bunch of folks out looking for us and we will be grounded in the house for a month." Adam yelled, "Why did we bring all this stuff with us if we didn't plan to stay in here for awhile, this doesn't make a bit of sense!"

After they rested awhile Motock asked, "Does anybody know which way is home?"

Everyone looked at each other not wanting to venture an answer. Then they started laughing. Adam replied, "We will just go back the way we came so all we have to do is turn around and go." It was really difficult to see anything as they walked along and fell over rocks and their faces getting all scratched up by low tree branches. They heard owls hooting and it was getting really spooky. It started to rain and there was thunder and lightening and the ground was getting really wet. There was a thick layer of soggy leaves on the forest floor and they fell down many times.

Motock and Bendbow were walking up ahead and all of a sudden they let out a yell and disappeared into the ground. They had fallen into a big hole or gully.

"Help, they yelled!"

Adam and Jacob couldn't tell how far down they were but it seemed to be pretty deep because their voices echoed as they called for help. Bendbow yelled, "The water is pretty deep down here it's almost to my knees." Jacob yelled back, "Can you tell how big the hole is, how wide or if there are any rocks you can climb on to get out of the water?"

"Yes!" Motock replied. There ain't any rocks but I can see enough to can get to the edges out of the water. The hole is pretty wide down here."

"Ok! We are going to look and see if we can find some vines that will reach down to you and pull you out. Wait a minute! Why are we looking for vines? We brought the rope!"

"Ok! You guys try and see if you can get under where my voice is coming from so we can lower the rope to you. We will tie a small branch on the end so you can get hold of it."

It took what seemed forever for Motock to yell out that he had finally found the rope. Adam yelled out to them, "I am going to wrap the rope around my waist and we will pull you up. Let me know when you have a good hold on the rope."

Both Adam and Jacob started pulling, the ground was very wet and the leaves were really slippery. They pulled and all of a sudden they lost their footing and they both slid right down into the hole with Motock and Bendbow.

"Now that's just great! We are all down here now and no way to get out!" yelled Jacob. "We better go around the edges and see if we can find a cave or an over hang to get out of this rain and water."

The hole was a whole lot bigger than they imagined and they finally found a cave or what appeared to be a cave. It was very dark and musty smelling and damp but at least they were out of the rain and water. They had no intentions of going further back into the cave not knowing what might be in there or if there were tunnels leading from it for them to get lost in. Adam had sprained his ankle in the fall and seemed to be in a lot of pain. Jacob told the boys that he thought he had heard the dogs Rondo, Rebel and Rubbish out hunting.

Immediately the boys all started yelling the dog's names hoping they weren't too far away to hear. In a surprisingly short time they could hear the dogs baying as they ran through the woods. Then as they looked up into the darkness and rain they could hear panting. The dogs had found them. "Rebel, Rondo, Rubbish, go home! Go home!" shouted Adam. The dark, rain drenched air above settled over them. Now all they could do is wait and hope the dogs had gone home and that someone would come looking for them.

Ashley and Melanie returned home around time for supper to find Biddy and Wylie Clegg and Old Wiggins frantically running in circles in a panic. They had not been able to find the boys and no one had seen them since after breakfast. From one of the neighboring ranchers Ashley found out he thought they had gone to Spook Owl Mountain. One of the local Indian boys had come by and asked if he could borrow some fishing gear.

Ashley was furious since he had told the boys on more than one occasion that he did not want them going there on their own, that it was not safe and they didn't know their way around and what if they got lost or injured. How would anyone know where to come looking for them?

Fearing the worst Ashley got the men together and saddled the horses and took a few for the boys just in case. There were just too many places and ways they could get into trouble. They could fall into ravines and drown caused by the run off from the rain.

Before they even got started they heard the dogs coming in a distance barking and howling like the devil was after them. When the dogs reached them they stopped and kept turning in circles, barking and running off a short distance then coming back trying to get the men to follow them. After a minute or two the men got the message, spurred their mounts and went galloping through the pasture toward the mountain. The hounds were out front, barking as they ran.

Once they got to the bottom of the mountain they tied off the horses to some trees and took off on foot with the dogs in the lead. The going was pretty slow because of the muddy ground. There were holes and stumps and logs that they had to be careful not to fall over. They brought lanterns, water and rope and anything else they thought would be helpful. After about two hours they finally found the hole and the boys were yelling to get their attention once they heard the dogs barking and coming in their direction.

Ashley yelled down into the hole, "Looks like you boys managed to get yourselves into a fine mess. Now all we have to do is figure out how to get you all out of there." Jacob yelled back as he looked up into the dim light that filtered down into the hole.

"Adam has a sprained ankle and can't walk on it and it's hurting bad he says. Motock and Bendbow are also down here."

"We will throw down some ropes and bring you up one at a time," Ashley told them. "When you get the rope, tie it around each of Adam's legs right above the knee so it looks like a sling and hang on while we pull you up." That worked out well and soon Adam was up at the top on the ground moaning over his sore ankle. The other three boys were easier to get up. They tied the rope around their waists and walked up the side of the hole as the men pulled them up.

When everyone was rescued Ashley announced," We should all sit here and rest a bit and then head home, your Mother has been worried sick and I am certain both Motock and Bendbow's mothers are also extremely worried not knowing where they are. I had one of the men go over to their camp and talk to their fathers and have them at the ranch waiting for them when we get back. They will probably whip them all the way back home. I don't know how many times I have told you boys not to come here to this mountain and still you disobeyed me so there will be some repercussions and punishments when you get back home. We will talk about that tomorrow after your Mother gets through with you." The boys looked at each other and knew what that meant.

On the way back to Harmony the boys were told to ride up in front where they could be watched. They rode in silence totally embarrassed by their failed adventure and to make it worse they had to listen to their father and the ranch hands as they talked and laughed quietly as they rode behind them.

"It was just plain lucky those dogs knew where to find them. You would think they had treed a bobcat they way they carried on when they found the hole the boys were in." As Ashley shook his head he said, "I certainly wouldn't want to be in their shoes when their Mother gets a hold of them. Of course we never did anything like that when we were growing up did we?" asked Ashley as he winked an eye at the ranch hands.

As with most things in life children survive a Mother's tough love. After getting a severe warning and a few well-placed hands on their butts from their father the boys grew into manhood with a renewed sense of discipline and when their father died of complications caused by pneumonia they stayed at the ranch to take care of it and their Mother. Margaret continued with her teaching, graduated from college, moved away from Harmony and into a small house in Atlanta. The years passed quickly and every Saturday morning she returned to Harmony but only long enough to get a few of the ranch hands to go out riding with her.

Chapter Eight

The Southeastern United States in the early 1800's especially around the cotton mills of Georgia and Tennessee were a hive of bustling activity. Industrialization of the mills and the invention of the cotton gin by Eli Whitney in 1793 had virtually doubled and in some instances tripled production. Along with industrialization came the usual scalawags and carpetbaggers seeking to make a quick profit often at the expense of an unwary traveler or businessman. The cotton mill found its beginnings in Lancashire England where approximately eighty percent of the world's cotton was processed before 1825. William determined to change that and bring an industrialized America into the picture.

Cotton mills or sweatshops as they were sometimes called were basically truck farms based on the company store system where the workers bought their food, clothing and bare necessities on credit. After the company store bill was paid very little if any money was left over. Debt bondage was common. The common wage of seventy-five cents a week was paid for more genteel types of employment such as housemaids. In the factories the wage was a little higher but with it came physical and verbal abuse. The factory girl was the lowest among women to be beaten, pinched and degraded if she did not perform her job properly according to her overseer. Typically a woman in 1830 had no property rights and was not supposed to be able to handle any type of financial arrangement. A husband could in effect declare her an encumbrance to his estate and leave her penniless at his death.

The Boott cotton mills at Lowell Massachusetts represented the best of textile mills. It used both water and steam power and at any given time during the day sounds of rumbling machinery and bells clanging regulated the day's work. William owned four cotton mills in and around Atlanta Georgia but today he was in Lowell to talk to Mr. Kirk Bott about a tour of his company and possibly get some new insights into expansion of his own mills.

He had to admit he felt slightly intimidated as he stood in the courtyard of the Boott textile mills. The massive walls stood over him like a medieval castle or great church cathedral. Thick red brick walls punctuated by glass windows of many sizes and shapes rose from the ground. The wall separated the courtyard from the Merrimack River. Within the courtyard the surrounding spaces could only be entered across one single bridge. Brick and wooden stair towers provided the only means of entering the upper floors. A single bell tower dominated the entire courtyard. As he stood there someone came across the courtyard and went up into the bell tower. Shortly afterwards the bell chimed three times and within minutes the entire courtyard was a mass of people leaving the buildings. William stood at the entrance to the bell tower and waited for the man to come down.

"Sir, if I could trouble you as to where I might find Mr. Kirk Boott?"

"He would be in his office this time of day," the man answered.

"And could you direct me to where that is?"

"I can do better than that me laddy, I will take you meself."

The man's thick Irish brogue was a little hard to understand at first but as they chatted it became easier.

"Excellent," said William, "Is the bell only rang once a day?"

"Oh no, several times as a matter of fact," responded the man as he smiled. "There is the morning bell at the start o' the shift, then the mid day bell for the meal break then the shift end to go home bell."

"I see, thank you. It was most informative. Mr. Boott if you would please?"

"Won't be but a wee minute's walk, Mr...?" The man had guessed William to be a few years younger than him but his clothes spoke of being a gentleman and a very rich one at that.

"Claibourne, William Claibourne."

They stood at the base of the bell tower and waited for the throngs of people to thin out. It was impossible to guess at the number but certainly in the hundreds, perhaps thousands. "Follow me if you please?" asked the man as he motioned with his arm towards one of the massive walled buildings. Inside the building on the second floor the man discretely knocked on a solidly built wooden door. "Yes?" came a voice from within the room. "Mr. Boott a William Claibourne to see ye Sir."

"Come in, come in. Finley would you bring us some tea."

"Yes, Sir. Right away."

"Have a seat Mr. Claibourne," said Mr Boott as he motioned to the chair in front of his desk. "You have several mills around Atlanta, correct?"

William was surprised he knew of his holdings but chose to not show it. "Yes and thank you for receiving me on such short notice. I have five mills at the present and business has been fairly good, however I am always open to new ideas and would appreciate a tour of your mills here if that is possible?"

"Certainly. Perhaps we can learn from each other. I understand you pay your people an hourly wage instead of a weekly?"

"You are well informed Mr. Boott. Yes, I do and give then Sunday off as well to attend to personal and religious things."

"Hmmm," said Mr. Boott as he furrowed his brow and stroked his chin. "And you still make a very hefty profit. Do you intend on expanding your holdings soon?"

"Yes, perhaps in a year or two." William sensed he was getting a little too personal and decided to not give away too much information until he knew the man better. Finley had arrived with the tea and sat the huge tray down on the desk between them. "That will be all Finley," said Mr. Boott as he reached across the desk and poured the tea into two heavy cups. "Sugar, cream?" he asked.

"Sugar, two please."

The two of them sat, drank two cups of hot tea and talked for the better part of an hour. Mr. Boott, William learned was a shrewd businessman and also believed in treating his people fairly. He liked the man and knew he could learn a lot. After tea Finley came and took the tray away. Then the two of them spent the remainder of the day walking through the mill. William was most impressed in the amount of lighting and fresh air provided by the open windows. He also learned heat was provided in the winter months by a massive system of piping and steam boilers. Up until that time the Boott mills were the epitome of textile manufacturing. Late in the afternoon they sat in the upstairs office and again Finley brought tea and pastries for the two of them. William had learned a lot from Mr. Boott. As he sat in his boat cabin on the return trip to Atlanta he knew expansion plans into Tennessee had to be completed very quickly.

After returning to Atlanta William decided to quickly buy up as many textile mills around Atlanta, Savannah, Charleston and New Orleans as he could. He had seen what good management could do plus he had a few ideas of his own. He would build his own textile empire hopefully before Mr. Boott became aware of his plans and took steps to prevent it. Tennessee was a little too far north to expand his business there as yet but William knew eventually he would move there because that was where good cotton grew and land was cheap.

It seemed new things were being done and invented every day. In February up north in Pennsylvania the first coal burning locomotive had made its first trial run. In New York a steam engine train made a run from Albany to Schenectady. There was even a rumor of someone in England inventing a machine to cut grass. On the other side of progress there were several news items that greatly disturbed William. In Virginia a slave named Nat Turner led a revolt that ended with over fifty white people being killed. Turner was later captured, hanged and then skinned but clearly unrest and slavery issues were in the air. William employed many Negroes in his mills and cotton fields but they were free to leave at any time.

The year was 1831 and winter had already taken a firm hold on the south. In a few months the New Year would be celebrated but all was not cheerful in spite of the streets of Atlanta being decorated with red, green and silver strands still left over from the holidays. A newspaper in Norfolk Virginia had carried an article about Nat Turner's revolt. As William read the article that was quoted in a local newspaper he felt in his heart the south was in turmoil over the slavery issue.

According to the article Turner felt led by an act of God because he saw a halo around the sun. William knew of atrocities that had been carried out by many slave owners because they felt their slaves weren't working fast enough, were disrespectful or just plain lazy. Many plantation owners were fearful Turner's revolt would lead to many more such instances and often demanded protection from their local government. Militia units from the surrounding areas descended on Jerusalem, Virginia and a massacre of blacks began. Much of this torture and killing of Negroes was done by vigilante group's intent on revenge. Hundreds of blacks were killed even though many were totally innocent of any involvement or even knew of Nat Turner's rebellion. Clearly the slavery issue was becoming a major problem in Southern America.

The years went by quickly and William traveled extensively going from cotton plantations to textile mills often buying them very cheaply because the news of slavery issues were almost on every newspapers front page. At the same time he was buying plantations and cotton mills William was buying land in Tennessee. If all went as planned he would move north in nine or ten years.

William's stepfather had impressed upon him the value and importance of being dependent only upon himself to get things done. Since that time when he had stood at the ship's rail with the storm's fury lashing at his body he had not allowed his feelings to interfere with business or relations with anyone. That had been twelve long years ago but now he realized he needed someone to share his life with. Sure he had been to many parties and balls when it suited his needs to seal a business deal but hardly ever for the sheer pleasure of being around people. There was a New Year's party set for two months away perhaps he could go and start learning about people if it wasn't too late.

Everyone was expected to go in costume but he had no idea what or who to go as. His houseman, Jarvis suggested he go as frontiersman and wear leather buckskins. William liked the novelty of the idea and asked if he knew any place such an outfit may be purchased? "Yes, Sir," Jarvis answered, " Most any good order catalogue has them. I will attend to it Mr. William."

The evening of the costume ball William was standing on the balcony overlooking a massive and very beautiful garden when a young couple came out of the ballroom to get a breath of fresh air. He guessed them to be slightly younger than himself. He was at one end of the garden balcony and standing in the shadows. The young couple stood very close to each other face to face then as he watched they stole a quick kiss and then turned to look out over the garden. William realized he had been too involved in business to take any time for personal matters such as a wife. He wanted a family but business had always come first, until now. The young couple went back inside the ballroom leaving William to stand alone in the darkness.

Two weeks later William had Jarvis drive him into town in the open carriage. Winter was already in full swing but this morning the air was unseasonably warm. The locals sometimes referred to it as Indian summer but that was usually earlier in the year.

"Jarvis I'll be seeing a man about buying a riding horse this morning so just put the buggy in the livery stable. I shouldn't be more than an hour or so."

"Yes Sir, Mr. William. There is a Mr. Jenkins over at the bank who I am told has Morgan's but doesn't want a pile of gold for them."

"Thank you. Morgan's you say? That's a fine breed of horse. Good sturdy, can run all day, does well in the mountains."

"Yes Sir. Good luck."

As William walked the few steps from the livery to the bank four mounted horsemen slowly rode by and dismounted in front of the saloon. Three of them went in and the other one went into the general store. William guessed he probably needed some chewing tobacco. At the bank William introduced himself to the teller and asked to see Mr. Jenkins.

"Mr. Jenkins I understand you have Morgans for sell?"

"Yes Sir, Mr. Claibourne. Yes, Mr. Claibourne I didn't recognize the name as having a current account with the bank."

"You are correct. I transferred my account to a bank in Memphis a month ago."

"If I may ask, was something not satisfactory with the services here?"

"No, the bank's services are excellent but I plan to move to Tennessee very shortly and that is confidential information Mr. Jenkins."

"I completely understand. As for a horse I do have Morgan's for sale. I bought a stud from Mr. Justin Morgan himself five years ago sired by Figure. I just sold one to a Mr. Ashley last month. Sort of a odd name for a cattleman but that's all I know about him. He said it was a present for his daughter because she didn't like the one he had given her a number of years back. Said it was too high spirited for her to handle on the cattle drives."

"A girl on a cattle drive?" asked William.

"Yes, it does sound a little strange doesn't it," said Mr. Jenkins as he chuckled. "I am told she is quite a hand full. Just last week she entered a rifle shooting contest and beat over a dozen men."

"Sounds like quite a girl."

William thanked the banker for the information and after signing the deed for the horse he left the bank, went outside and crossed the street to get something to eat at the local boarding house, which was right beside the general store. Just as he opened the door to go in the boarding house he noticed a rider holding the reins and had one foot in the stirrup to mount the horse. From the back the rider looked too small to be a man so William figured it was a boy. The horse was compactly muscled at the shoulder and had an expressive face, large eyes, well-defined withers, a well-arched neck and a clean-cut head. It stood at least fourteen hands. William realized he was looking at a Morgan.

"Excuse me son, isn't that a little too much horse for you to be riding?" asked William.

"No, I don't think so at all," said the rider and turned to face William.

As soon as the rider turned to face him he realized a mistake had been made. The rider was a girl or woman rather and a very beautiful one at that.

" I apologize miss, I mean Mamn. Your back was turned and I naturally assumed…"

"You assumed because I was riding a big horse and I am wearing pants that I was a man?"

"Uh Yes. Again I deeply apologize."

"Don't you think women can ride as good as a man, can shoot as good as a man or do you think they should just stay home cook and have babies?" she asked as she smiled and chuckled lightly. She was having fun and at William's expense but somehow it didn't seem she was laughing at him but at his idea of what a woman was supposed to be. He was completely flustered and for the first time in his life at a complete loss for words. He was used to dealing with hardened businessmen to get what he wanted but just in the short space of a few minutes this very beautiful young lady had completely disarmed him, he was defenseless and he realized he was in love.

Finally he found his voice and asked, " I don't know how to answer that question except to ask if you would marry me?"

"Well, that is not exactly what I was expecting but apology accepted and yes I will."

Chapter Nine

The engagement announcement party had been a tremendous success and well over a hundred people attended. The party came as a surprise put together by his ladylove. How she managed to invite so many folks without him knowing about it was simply amazing. She had even found many of the people he had done business with for the last few years and when they stood in line to shake their hands at the front door he greeted each of them warmly and thanked them for coming. Even some who he had been close to ruthless with in getting the deal he wanted smiled genuinely and complimented him on finding such a gracious host as his fiancé.

As the guests shook each of their hands and wished them well on their marriage William glanced down the line and there was one gentleman who looked very familiar. He could not remember his name or from where he knew him. Finally he stood in front of William and offered his hand. "It's your turn and I believe you have one question left," he said as he smiled broadly.

"One question?" asked William as he furrowed his brow in puzzlement then said loudly, "Nathan, Nathan Guilderhouse!" as he took both of Nathan's hands in his in a strong two-handed handshake.

"In the flesh, William. How long has it been since the boarding school?"

"Ten years? Has it been that long?" asked William in amazement.

"Yes. My father has since died of pneumonia and Mother is suffering terribly from some ailment the doctors don't know anything about. Doctors are all a bunch of amateurs and quacks and don't deserve any of their vaunted reputations."

"I quite agree. I seriously think they come up with most of their medical answers by looking into a crystal ball."

"Yes, it does seem that way at times, doesn't it? I have been hearing good things about your cotton mills ventures."

"Yes, I have been extraordinarily propitious and Lady Luck smiles on me at times."

"I don't think luck has anything to do with it William. Even in school you always had a good head on your shoulders and always seemed to know exactly what you wanted out of life and it was just a matter of time getting it."

"Even so," replied William, " I can use a good man. Would you be interested in a partnership?"

"I am sure it would be an excellent and profitable endeavor but I must decline for personal reasons."

"All the same, please think on it and we can talk later after dinner."

While the two of them had been standing and talking the remainder of the guests stood patiently waiting their turn understanding the feelings expressed by old friends meeting again after many years.

William did consider himself very lucky in finding Margaret and even more fortunate when she said yes to his marriage proposal. He greatly admired her directness and in the short time they had known each other he realized how much he loved her. Usually with people of the fairer disposition and even with a few mature ladies he had been most courteous and treated them with a little less respect than with businessmen. With Margaret, however that all changed and he found making himself available to do whatever she needed doing. It left him feeling good inside. If that was what people called being in love then he had it badly and welcomed it.

When the last person had passed through the reception line and congratulated them William mingled through the crowd and found Nathan. "So what have you been doing with yourself for the last ten years?" William asked.

"Oh, nothing much to brag about actually, few business deals that went badly because I trusted the managers and overseers a little too much. I did find a wonderful lady, however and get married. We have two children, a boy and a girl. My father trusted me again before he died and sold me one of his mills at a rock bottom price. He said the reason he sold it to me instead of as an inheritance was so I would appreciate its value more"

"Congratulations on both the marriage and the children. It sounds like you have a promising future ahead of you. I do wish you would reconsider my offer as a partner."

"It is indeed tempting and I am sure in a short amount of time it would be very profitable but the reason I must decline is your standpoint on slavery. You do not see the black man as a slave and something of value to be owned but as a person."

"We are all human beings Nathan. Some are a little more privileged than others and others a little more intelligent but that doesn't mean we cannot respect anyone less because of their circumstances."

"A valid point but I sincerely don't think it would work between us as a partnership. Thank you for the offer and give your lovely fiancé my best."

"I will do that Nathan and thank you."

Later that evening after all the guests had left and there were only himself, Margaret and a few servants cleaning up left in the house. William asked Margaret if she thought his standpoint on slavery was unusual?

"No, I don't think it is unusual at all. Slavery is more commonly traditional in the south as a way of life but that doesn't mean you have to accept it as being normal everywhere. There are whites that aren't any better than the Negro as far as station in the community, manners and finances and some Negroes that are far better businessmen than whites in the northern states."

Margaret's explanation of the way some things are done left him feeling at ease and he took her in his arms and said, "You are absolutely amazing with your philosophy on life. My stepfather taught me to respect everyone, to a certain degree of course and to try and find some good in everyone but you have carried that to a finer point than I ever could. I think that is why I love you so much. No, I don't think, I know that is why I love you."

The two of them stood in the middle of the spacious living room with their arms wrapped around each other oblivious of the servants as they went about the business of cleaning up. They completely lost track of time until William noticed there were no sounds in the house. The servants had all left and they were alone. "Where do you want to go for our honeymoon?" William asked.

"An around the world tour, Paris, London, the Far East and after that New Orleans, New York and San Francisco," Margaret answered with a mischievous grin as she looked into his eyes. "Your wish is my command my Lady Love," said William as he made a deep bow. "Seriously William a world tour would be fabulous but all I really want is somewhere very private for just the two of us and no servants but I think your father is planning a big party at his ranch."

"Yes, I know but I think we can sneak off during the excitement, it's traditional."

" I think we should discuss where we want to live and raise our family. I feel there is trouble in the wind about this slavery issue and it might be a good idea to consider somewhere that is a little more favorable. Perhaps somewhere in the northern region?"

"Or better yet somewhere that is neutral to both sides."

"You do believe in fairy tales don't you?' said William as he held her close in his arms.

"No, actually but if trouble is inevitable why take either side?"

"Someplace neutral sounds like Tennessee. I hear land is very cheap and we could sell what we have here and move. If trouble does arise over this slavery issue it would not be for a few years I am sure and we would already be set up on our own land. Cotton is always a good commodity to invest in."

"Tennessee it is then. What about servants and field hands? I am an excellent cook and do not need any help in the kitchen but if we are to have a family I will need someone to lift the heavy things when the time comes."

"Servants, yes, and as for field hands I will not own a slave. If we have to have field hands they will be there of their own free will the same as a factory worker and will be paid a going wage. A family, yes, I do want children but not if they have to grow up in a time of war."

"You realize if there is war it may come to us whether we like it or not."

"Yes, it may very well be but that is surely some years away. So let's plan for moving to Tennessee after the honeymoon."

"Yes, Tennessee it is."

Chapter Ten

Ashley and Melanie while sitting on the verandah having their morning coffee seemed deep in thought.

"Sweetheart now that we have the engagement party out of the way it's time we started preparing for the wedding there is a great deal to do."

"I suppose you are right. Have you talked with Margie about where they would like the wedding to take place?"

"Honey, she has her heart set on having the wedding right here at Harmony in their special place down by the creek facing the mountains." "She told me that it has always been their special place. They love to sit under the weeping willow in the shade and watch the pair of Swans that you bought for her. I believe they have named them Angel and Cowpoke." "I have also talked with Pastor McDaniel and he will be very pleased to officiate.

"I think that is a great idea, then the guests won't have far to travel."

"We can erect a large tent just in case it should rain and we can have the reception right here as well and since we planned on having a large BBQ we can join the two, the party and the reception."

Ashley sat back in his chair and sighed. He was very happy at the thought of his daughter getting married. He could almost see the wheels turning in Melanie's head while considering all the things that would need to be done in a short time.

He suddenly sat bolt upright and asked. "By the way when have they decided the wedding should be?"

Melanie replied. " We have one month to prepare and get everything done." "Biddy and her crew in the kitchen have been buying goods for a couple of weeks now knowing what was coming in the future."

Ashley smiled and said, "leave it to Biddy she is always way ahead of us when it comes to these kinds of events."

Melanie responded with a couple of deep sighs and said, " Well at least someone is way ahead of us. Margie and I have to make a trip to Atlanta to find her wedding dress. Margie is determined to have a Paris wedding gown and that's the only place we will find one short of going to Paris."

Ashley, laughing replied, "I'd say the two of you had better get cracking then, time is a wasting. I will speak with Old Wiggins and have him get the coach ready for the trip and if all goes well you can go on this weekend. You probably won't need more than a day to get her gown and her trousseau. So if you leave here on Wednesday of next week if all goes well you should arrive in Atlanta by Monday morning." " I better get with Margie and get things ready for the trip before she makes any other plans for parties." "She may want her best friend Lynette to go with us."

Margie was all but jumping for joy when Melanie told her of their up and coming trip to buy her wedding gown and trousseau. "Oh! Momma can we really go to Atlanta?" "Yes, darling, nothing but the best for my only lovely daughter." "Your Father would not have it any other way, in fact it was his suggestion." "I am the luckiest girl in the whole wide world."

William and Margie were sitting under the weeping willow tree having their basket lunch they brought with them talking about their wedding and up coming honeymoon. Margie looking at William lovingly said, "Sweetheart, do you really want to know where I would love to spend our honeymoon? Where is that my love? You will truly think I have lost my mind when I tell you but I have been thinking about it for the longest time. I want us to go to the cottage up in the mountains by the lake. It's quiet and peaceful and we can be truly alone without any distractions. You know how much I love to swim and lay out in the sun and with you by my side nothing could be more perfect. Besides, I can pleasure you with my cooking and we can finally realize what our life together will be like and there will be nothing or no one to interrupt us." "I think that is a wonderful idea Margie and I will have you all to myself and it will be like we are the only two people in the whole world."

The whole month had been a whirlwind of activity. Melanie and Margie had gone to Atlanta and spent a whole day trying on and looking at gowns. They brought the sizes of the bridesmaids and maid of honor along with them to make sure they had everything just right. Melanie's wedding gown looked as though it had been made for a princess. It was a beautiful gown in the style of a ball gown with layers and layers of imported lace. Since it was summer all the bridesmaid's gowns were pastel colored in shades of purple and lavender. Her train was not exceptionally long since the wedding was outside and would have been cumbersome.

The bunkhouse crew and Old Wiggins and Charlie were busy getting the gardens prepared along with a lattice canopy covered with flowers for the bride and groom and the Pastor to stand under. The pathway would be sprinkled with rose petals on the day of the wedding. The wedding itself was set for late afternoon so that they would not have to deal with the hot rays of the sun and Margaret especially wanted pedestals with candles to light the way down the path to the canopy and the Pastor. The men also had to go out to the woods and make sure they had enough wood chopped for the grills.

The kitchen was a flurry of activity getting all the meat prepared for the grills and the salads made as well as the biscuits and cookies and of course the wedding cake. Margaret and William's wedding day finally arrived with brilliant rays of the sun and no sign of a single cloud in the sky. Everyone was busy getting everything ready for later in the afternoon.

Margie was sitting in the bay window of her bedroom looking out at the scene and all the frenzy of activity going on. She was beginning to get a bit nervous that by the end of this day she would be Mrs. William Claibourne and wondered if she would feel different as a person knowing she would have so much responsibility, more than she had ever known in her life before. Pretty soon Lynette would get here and they would have to start getting bathed and ready and she knew that time would just fly by. She could see that some guests who had to travel from afar already started to arrive.

Just then Lynette came flying through the door laughing and yelling with excitement. "Oh Margie! I am so excited I don't know what to do with myself! Pretty soon you will be an old married woman and I will be alone with no one to talk to. Margie just looked at her smiling and saying "My goodness Linnie I'm not dying, I'm just getting married so calm down before you make me crazy."

Ashley was standing by the window in the bedroom half dressed and feeling a bit sorry for himself as Melanie came into the room from the bathroom. "What's the long face for dear?" she asked. "I am losing my little girl, she won't need her daddy anymore honey," responded Ashley. "If that isn't the silliest thing I have ever heard darling, Margie will always need her mother and father. She isn't going to just disappear and not see her brothers

Adam and Jacob and us, not to mention those silly dogs and the cats." "Of course sweetheart you are right."

Just as the sun went down in the western sky the sound of the organ playing the wedding march began. First the bridesmaids walked along the pathway toward the canopy where the Pastor and William and his best man stood waiting. Then came Margie an angelic gorgeous Madonna figure whose feet appeared to not even be touching the ground as she floated slowly down the pathway toward her love and her future. She was trembling as she handed her bouquet to her maid of honor and took William's hand. His heart was overwhelmed by her beauty and grace as he smiled at her and kissed her hand.

The vows said and the blessings made William and Margie turned to face their family and friends while rice flew everywhere and the party and dancing would begin. Ashley said, "May I now announce Mr. and Mrs. William Claibourne in their first dance toward their future as husband and wife."

The party lasted into the night with dancing and eating and merry making but as time went by no one seemed to notice that the bride and groom were no longer with them. Margie and William had taken the carriage all decorated with flowers and boughs up into the mountain to the cottage on the lake and as they sat on some rocks looking out at the moon and stars and the water listening to the night birds they drank their first toast to each other as husband and wife.

Margie appeared in the bathroom door leading into the bedroom in a sheer white nightgown with the moon shining through the window behind her and walked into the arms of her husband for the first time. With their mouths fused and their bodies melted together, his hands curved under her bottom and lifted her off the floor as he carried her the rest of the way into the bedroom to their bridal bed. He set her down slowly, and she slid against him. meeting the hard urgency of his desire on her descent. Lifting heavy eyelids, she looked up at him bewitchingly. She peeled the jacket off his shoulders and dropped it to the floor. She slipped the tie over his head and began taking off his shirt. He eased off his shoes with the toe of one foot on the heel of the other and kicked them aside.

When his shirt had joined the heap of clothes she playfully ran her fingertips over his nipples. They sprang to hard erectness under her touch. With direct slowness she leaned forward to kissed him and her tongue darted against his lips.

"Do you like that?" she whispered.

"Find out," he challenged.

She laid the back of her hand on his chest and slid it down slowly until her fingers went past his belt and into his trousers. He smiled smugly when she raised naughty eyes to his. Closing a fist around his buckle she began backing toward the double bed, dragging him with her.

"William! we are finally married and can really belong to each other heart and soul as one." She could only sigh his name as a familiar liquid fire began to seep through her body at his touch. She sat down on the side of the bed while he rid himself of pants and underwear. When he was standing before her with the magnificence of his form revealed. she rested her hand on the slight curve of his waist and leaned forward to press her lips against the silky shaft of hair at his abdomen. Their eyes worshipped each other surveying each other like a rare piece of sculpture created only for each other.

William lifting one arm up first, and then the other, kissed the insides of her elbows, finding erogenous places she didn't know she even possessed. She grabbed handfuls of his hair and imprisoned his head against her breasts. He wrested himself free.

"Shhh, not yet. Lie down." She had no energy to argue as he gently set her down. Her head tossed frantically on the pillow as his mouth continued its journey on her neck and then down to her stomach and breasts. Long moments passed while she swirled through a galaxy of uncharted bliss. It was all the better when he covered her body with his and tightly sheathed himself in the depths of her love. They soared above one universe and went on to the next, each one higher and brighter, until they reached the plane where spirits are united in an everlasting fire of love.

Replete, they clung together, marveling over the magnitude of the love they shared.

"I've been selfish. Forgive me for taking my time," he said quietly.

"There's one thing I hope you'll always be fiercely selfish about......your love for me," she whispered. He smiled and cuddled her close against him. "Of that you may be sure, my love. Of that you may be sure."

The full moon peeked through an open window to where they lay entwined naked in each other's arms. There was no shame. Their marriage bed was as it should be. Neither of them had known another before that night. Morning came and as the sun rose over the mountains William looked at the woman lying beside him and gently whispered, "I will always love and protect you. I will make the best life possible for us and our children and our children's children. This I swear."

Chapter Eleven

Margaret had just rang the bell signaling it was time for dinner. William looked down at his dirty fingernails and chuckled to himself. He could not remember the last time his hands had even been dusty much less covered in dirt. It was a good feeling to know the dirt came from his and Margaret's own land. The past three months had been filled with buying land in Tennessee along with the building materials for their new home. As he stood there and looked at the newly laid foundation and two story frame work for the main house he remembered the month long trip aboard the General Jackson steamboat up the Cumberland River.

The trip normally took a little over two weeks but he knew the Captain and immediately after the gangway had been pulled back from the dock at New Orleans he told Captain Wart this was to be his honeymoon. "A honeymoon you say?" asked the Captain.

"Yes," answered William," My new bride of only a few weeks and I plan to buy some land and settle somewhere around Nashville."

"Then may I suggest a gentleman by the name of Benjamin Morrissey who I understand has several large parcels south of Nashville and has a reputation of fairness and honesty."

"Thank you Captain. I will certainly take it under advisement."

"You are most welcome Mr. Claibourne and I will see to it personally that the trip will take a little longer than usual. I also extend my congratulations to yourself and the missus and it would be an honor if you would join me at my table for dinner every evening."

William knew it was a privilege to sit at the Captain's table and accepted the invitation. Captain Wart was a wealth of information about the Cumberland River and over several dinners he shared the information with his guests. The Riviere des Chauouanons was named by the French in 1670 for the Shawnee Indian tribe and later named the Cumberland by Dr. Thomas Walker.

In the very early years of the Cumberland's history during the Ice Age hunters used it to go around the glaciers north of the Ohio River to get to the vast game rich basin of the upper Cumberland. In the early 1700's continual wars between the Shawnee, Chickasaw and Cherokee Indian tribes made travel through the area dangerous except for the hardiest pioneers. Several tributaries of the Cumberland were named after early trappers and hunters including the Stones River for Uriah Stone and the Obey River for Obadiah Spencer.

The Cumberland was actually first chartered in 1769 by an army engineer by the name of Thomas Hutchins who referred to it as Shawanoe. Later in 1775 the Cumberland served as a border for the Transylvania Purchase a rather grand but risky venture by Richard Henderson.

In the early 1800's travel up and down the river was heavy due to increased crop productions of tobacco and cotton, which were sold in New Orleans. In 1819 the General Jackson made its debut in Nashville and began making regular runs up and down the river. Then finally in 1825 the Tennessee Legislation petitioned congress to survey the Cumberland and make the Cumberland the official shipping means between Nashville and New Orleans.

As the Captain continued his chatter about the Cumberland they dined on fresh caught fish, baked potatoes, corn on the cob, a salad with bits of small bread chunks, radishes and several types of greens and for desert there was fresh baked apple pie. With full stomachs they retired to their cabin for the evening.

During the daytime hours they strolled around the upper deck, arm in arm, and stopped often to stand at the ships rail and look at the riverbank over a half mile away gliding slowly by. The reds, golds and yellows of fall were in full bloom and it was a magnificent view. The Captain had loaned them his glass and as they looked through it they could spot deer and bear with their heavy winter coats among the trees. The bear were probably hurrying to find as much food as possible before hibernation for the winter and for the cubs that would be born during that time.

"Have I told you today I love you?" asked William as he took her hand in his while standing at the rail.

"No, you haven't but I know you do," answered Margaret.

"I admit when we sold everything in New Orleans and started out up river to Nashville I had reservations as to this being a good decision but now that we are on our way I feel it was the right thing to do. Your parents tried so hard to change our minds and stay at least until spring."

"Yes, mother was most adamant about staying and said we would get to Nashville and not be able to find a place to live and who did we know there in case something went wrong?"

William smiled to himself as he remembered the first few weeks of their arrival in Lindbergh. They had stayed in Nashville until William could arrange transportation to take them to their new home which was a good day or so journey southwest of there. They had to stay at the boarding house which was conveniently close to the bank and general store, both of which they would be needing later. True to his reputation Mr. Morrissey had a spread of a hundred acres of bottomland south west of Nashville. He asked how William had known bout him and when he mentioned Captain Wart a smile crossed his lips.

"So the old river pirate is still among the living?"

"Yes indeed and he sends his best regards to you and your family."

"We have been old friends for more years than I care to mention. He always did fancy the rivers and ocean. He said it was like the rivers flowed to the sea like our own blood flows to our hearts." An interesting analogy, William thought. In a very short period of time a deal was made for the land. They both went to the bank, money changed hands and a deed was signed. The next morning William hired a horse and buggy from a livery stable and during the two-hour ride they sat bundled up in blankets against the morning chill. William was very familiar with a team of horses and as he expertly flicked the rains over the horse's rumps he watched their frosty breaths as they trotted an easy gait. A slight smell of snow was in the air.

With the directions Mr. Morrissey had given him their land should be just around the next bend in the road. It wasn't an actual road; just two wagon tracks across the land but it served the purpose of getting from one place to another. There had not been very many things in William's life up to that moment to take his breath away but when they rounded the bend and saw the land in front of them all he could do was gasp and exhale very loudly.

The view was magnificent. Directly in front of them was a meadow area of about ten acres, perfectly flat, no trees and very little scrub brush. Beyond that the land sloped away slightly to merge in another flat grassy triangle with two small rivers. Mr. Morrissey had been true to his word. It was prime bottomland. Surprisingly there were only a few trees scattered here and there.

One massive oak tree caught his attention right away. It was standing to one side of the upper meadow and immediately William imagined he saw a three-story plantation house standing next to it. "Do you see what I see?" he asked Margaret. "If you mean the white four columned three story plantation house, yes. I do," she answered.

William and Margaret had been thinking about and dreaming of their new home for so long she sometimes wondered if it would ever happen. But it was happening and she was very happy. "Thank you dear," she said as she took one of his arms in hers and held it close to her body. The two of them stood there in the early morning arm in arm. Their breaths frosted in the chilled air as they stood together and finally climbed back into the buggy and rode back into town.

The land they chose to build on was perfect with a huge oak tree where the house would be built very near it. She could see it all in her minds eye. Further back there was a river where a very large weeping willow tree was growing. She knew already that this would be a favorite spot for her and planned her rose garden to be a little ways in front of it. She wanted to have footpaths and benches and hopefully a fountain. She could barely contain her excitement. It was quite a ways off before she would even get close to starting it with everything that would have to be done in the house. "I will just store it in my mind until the time comes," she said.

The move from Atlanta was hard on all of them. She knew that William was tired but wouldn't show it. He still had that nagging cough that worried her. The hands also were tired. They had so much lumber, brick, shingles and everything else it would take to build the house. There were also the four or five wagons with all the furniture that her mother insisted that she take with her. Most was Rosewood from her Grandmother's home and some from her Great-grandmother's home. After all that was the reason that it was so carefully taken care of all these years and there also some oriental rugs and many accessories for decorating. The last time her mother and father was in Paris they brought back some eloquent pieces and some beautiful Swarovski crystal chandeliers. She had both her grandmother's china dinnerware and servers and silver. She loved all the silk comforters and curtains and drapes that her mother carefully selected knowing her daughter's taste. Margie knew that William had this grand scheme for this house he was building and she hoped he would not be disappointed. He mentioned something like twenty-eight rooms. The thought of such a large house was overwhelming to her. How in the world will I ever keep it clean?

He was a perfectionist and there was only one way for him to do things and that was the right way with no shortcuts. There were to be the servant's quarters. They would require a very large kitchen and butlers pantry as well. There would have to be a great room and dinning room, library and Gentlemen's room for bourbon and those awful cigars. Of all the other rooms she had no idea. She laughed to herself. A man must have some time to himself and things that he can enjoy so she did not begrudge him. Oh, it just came to her about the bedroom and bathroom mirrors that her mother purchased in Paris and she hoped they packed them well.

Then there were the barns and the bunk houses for the men and stalls for the horses and of course the corrals for the hogs and pigs and steers and a smoke house. She wondered how in the world William would be able to keep all this straightened out in his mind with so very much to do.

Somewhere along the line they would have to check into a church so that when she had time she could participate in their activities, there were always things that needed doing for the poor and the children.

The wagons soon arrived and Margaret set about getting the hands to unload and place everything where she wanted it. Other wagons arrived almost daily with the other furniture, which William had purchased from that Judge in New York. They would certainly not have a bare house with all the furniture that was quickly arriving every day

Several ladies came by to apply for available jobs as well as a few gentlemen. Margaret hired Alice, a middle aged woman as cook. She previously worked for the Holcomb's at Manner House in Lindbergh and came with impeccable references. Then there was Portia who was quite young but she had a small daughter named Isabelle and Margaret thought Portia's appearance and manners were exceptional and Margie felt she would work out just fine as their maid.

She also hired several other ladies temporarily to help put up the drapes and curtains and place the linens and such. Alice might also need some help in the kitchen temporarily unpacking the dishes and all the other utensils. Margie considered several men that came by and applied for gardener and houseman as well as a handy man, and she took their information and would pass it on to William. She felt he should be the ones to interview and hire the men. He would be a much better judge of them than she would.

It was that same massive oak tree they were sitting under for the noon meal. When Margaret had rang the bell to quit work and wash up himself and about a dozen men and women gathered around the two tables covered with checkered table cloths. The men and their wives were townsfolk from Lindbergh whom William had hired to help with building their home and preparing the land for planting crops. After grace was said everyone sat down and began eating. The most colorful of the group was a mule driver or skinner as they were called who went by the name of Jim Bob.

Jim Bob owned the only pair of stump pulling mules in the county and he was always in demand. He was proud of his mules that he had affectionately named Bill and Jack They were huge, a matched pair, stood eighteen hands high and weighed over a thousand pounds each. William noticed before Jim Bob had washed up and sat down at the table he had both watered and fed his mules and as he stood in front of each one he reached up and stroked their long ears. They were his family. In the months that followed the routine of doing work on the house and preparing the land for crops kept everyone very busy. On a few occasions in the days that followed William noticed Margaret sit down at the table to catch her breath. He asked if she was feeling okay.

"What would you like?" she answered.

"For it to be spring, the summer crops planted and seeds ready for next years crops," he answered.

"No, I meant what would you like, a son or daughter?"

It took only a second for him to realize what his wife had asked him. "You mean….? Uh, a son. No, a daughter… either would be fantastic. Are you sure?"

"Yes, and I am sure it will be a daughter and she will be here late in December."

He was to be a father! Immediately he thought of working even harder to provide for his wife and the new arrival, to improve the temporary tent and lean to he had built for them to sleep in. At first he had insisted she stay in town at the boarding house until the house was completed but she argued if he could stay here in a tent so could she. Early on in their marriage he had learned it was best to not argue with his wife, at least not to loudly anyway.

She was of stern and strong pioneer stock and he was very proud of her.

One day, late in the summer as he was standing by the well that had just been finished, he realized the plantation needed a smoke house. He turned to look over the rows of white cotton that seemed to stretch forever down below and then back up toward the white columns of the plantation. He shaded his eyes against the bright mid day sun and saw two people standing at the gate by the road in front of the house. He had no idea how long they had been there.

As he walked up the hill he realized they were Negroes and as he got closer he noticed the height of the male and guessed it to be close to seven feet. The person next to him was also very tall and looked to be very much with child. William opened the black wrought iron gate and asked," Can I help you?"

"My husband can build it for you, just tell him where you want it." A look of puzzlement crossed his face and the woman added," Your smoke house. My husband can build it for you. There is plenty of hickory wood for the walls and clay down by the river for the bake ovens. He is a hard worker and very strong."

His amazement must have been very evident at her statement of her husband could build the smoke house because he had only thought of it a few minutes ago. He was also amazed of the precise and clear English she had used in her statement. He looked at the black giant that stood in front of him. He was taller than his own height of six feet seven and weighed at least two hundred sixty pounds but it was all lean muscle. He carried himself well and looked straight at him. There was no anger in his eyes just a look of poise. William had seen that look before and it was one of royalty but how could that be?

"I am Alaye Adesimbo and my wife is Asesimba Aminata," said the man in a very deep voice. "We come to America because of war in our countries of Nigeria and West Africa. We are travelers and need a place to stay until my son is born. I can build the house for you and a shelter for us and my son to stay in until we can continue our journey."

As William listened to the man he guess them to be political refugees. "I understand your situation completely and you can stay as long as you need."

"Thank you. My wife and I were mistaken for run away slaves and sold soon after we got off the boat but we ran away and now we fear they will find us again."

"I can have papers drawn up to the effect you belong to me but that is only a formality and at any time you may leave. Agreed?"

"It is agreed but for our safety we will only speak in very bad English if other people are around. Our names will be Sam and Sunshine."

"It is agreed," said William as he extended his hand. The black giant stood back a little unsure of the movement. "In America when a deal is made we shake hands," he explained. A broad smile lit up the giant's face to reveal two rows of surprisingly white teeth. "It is agreed," he said and took William's own not to small hand in one of his massively big ones. His grip could have easily crushed William's hand but instead it was one of friendship and trust. In a surprisingly short time the smoke and bake house were completed but before that a sturdy cabin was built for his wife and soon to be son.

Margaret's pregnancy was a hard one and the town doctor in Lindbergh was kept busy making numerous trips to check on her. After Sunshine had gave birth to a son she began staying close to Margaret and helping any way she could which often consisted of making meals, cleaning and tending to the needs of Margaret. She also spent many hours in the cookhouse baking biscuits, bread and cakes. The heat and smoke from the two clay bake ovens provided a means of cooking and preserving the meat stored high in the smoke house rafters. Almost daily it seemed someone would come by the front gate to trade a clean killed deer, bear or small varmint for a warm loaf of fresh baked bread or a handful of bear sign sprinkled with sugar. Sunshine was a shrewd trader and always got the best of the deal.

The doctor had been with Margaret most of the day in one of the downstairs bedrooms. It was early evening and she had been in labor for almost ten hours. William nervously paced the floor outside the bedroom waiting for some kind of word as to how Margaret was doing. Occasionally Sunshine, who was acting as helper and midwife would come out and tell him more hot water was needed. As he returned with the fourth pan of very hot water and placed his hand on the doorknob to let him in the bedroom a loud wail rang through the halls of the plantation to announce the arrival of his new child. Throwing the pan of water aside he rushed into the room to see the doctor wiping the blood from a small bundle in his hands. "Congratulations," he said, "You have a fine and healthy daughter." Then he gently gave his daughter to his wife. William quickly went over and knelt down at her bedside. "I present our daughter, Elizabeth," said Margaret as she uncovered the small head now nursing at her breast. "I love you," he said, "And I vow to make a good home for us, our children and their children."

"She needs rest," said the doctor, "The midwife can tend to her needs much better now than we can."

"Yes and thank you doctor. I will be in town in a few days to settle up."

"That would be wonderful Mr. Claibourne. I will see myself out."

Not often did William smoke or drink but the thought of a cigar and whiskey seemed appropriate for the occasion. After getting a cigar from the box he kept on his desk in the study and a small glass of whiskey from a cabinet in the kitchen he went back up stairs and sat outside the bedroom on the verandah in an old chair he had saved from being burned as scrap. It was now full evening and the stars were twinkling high in the black sky. The air was clean, cold, crisp and smelled faintly of smoke from the cookhouse as an errant breeze wafted by. As he sat there a few brave snowflakes fell slowly to land on the blanket that covered his legs.

He was not a soft man but at the thought of everything that had happened to himself over the last eighteen months, his new bride, and a fresh start here in Tennessee and now the birth of his daughter, he realized he was a blessed man. He closed his eyes as a moment of emotion took him and tears flowed down his cheeks. "Thank you Lord," he said reverently. It was Christmas Eve.

Chapter Twelve

The year was 1858 and it was Elizabeth's thirteenth birthday. The air was filled with chatter and festivities. It seemed like every one of Lindbergh's nine hundred and two citizens were there to celebrate the occasion. Sunny had baked several cakes and decorated them with candy sweets from the general store in town. Glasses filled with apple cider were raised in a toast. William's voice carried over all the others as he said, "To our daughter, Elizabeth!" Not only was that night a celebration of Elizabeth's birthday but it was also the end of a bumper crop of cotton that had already been shipped down river to New Orleans to be sold.

For the past ten years every cotton crop had been a little better than the one before because of new methods of utilizing fertilizer and alternating the harvest every other year with corn. Eli Whitney had invented the cotton gin some sixty-five years before and it vastly aided in the harvest and yield of cotton crops. The addition of a corn crop every other year not only helped to replenish the nutrients in the soil but the corn itself was a great delight. The townsfolk often came by the plantation to fill their bushel baskets with ears of corn and leave in trade fresh vegetables from their own gardens. Beef was a luxury commodity few had to spare so venison and small game were often used as barter for corn seed. Even after all the corn was harvested, the bartering and eating done there was still plenty of seed to ship down river.

With the inventions of the cotton gin and the steam engine farming had become quite commercialized and prosperous. With six corn crops and seven of cotton the banker in Lindbergh was very glad when harvesting time was over and the crops were sold in New Orleans because that meant a large amount of money would be deposited in his bank. He knew being a relatively small bank in a small town it was an easy target for robbers. So he went to New York and purchased a Diebold Cannonball safe, which was advertised as the best way to prevent robbers from making a midnight withdrawal or a withdrawal of any kind.

The safe's combination was set so that it could only be opened in daylight hours thus thwarting any attempt of robbers to keep the banker overnight and force him to open it at first light. The safe's weight of over 3,500 pounds was also a major deterrent to any foolhardy robber who was considering hauling it away on a wagon to be blasted open at their leisure. The bank manager had the safe shipped by freight wagon to arrive in broad daylight so all the townsfolk could see when it was unloaded. A set of heavy-duty pulleys was used to lift the safe off the wagon and lower it onto a row of solid oak rollers. From there six men easily pushed it into the bank. The manager figured it would be good advertisement for everyone to see how heavy it was and hopefully word would spread to thiefs and deter any thoughts of robbing the bank

The evening was almost a complete success. The only thing to spoil an otherwise perfect celebration was a somewhat unruly and very intoxicated gentleman who owned the hotel and dance hall in town. Somehow he managed to catch William as he was going into the kitchen for more cake to add to the two that had already been set out. Fortunately Sunshine had spent the better part of two days baking several types of cakes and deserts for the occasion. The gentleman's breath was heavy with liquor as he stood in front of William and argued that he thought he was a fool for being so lax in his handling of slaves. William quickly set him straight by telling him any black people on his property were his employees, not his slaves. They were free to leave at any time but chose to stay of their own free will.

"There is trouble in the wind," continued the intoxicated businessman, "Northerners are stirring up politics to free the blackies and make them as good as us."

"Everyone has a right to live as they please," said William, " Without being considered any lesser than anyone else just because of situations in their life. From what I understand the Negroes did not have a choice in coming to America but were basically kidnapped by slavers from their homeland and brought here to be sold at market."

"Even so, I cannot bring myself to think of them the same as us, let alone human beings. If the southerners want to keep their slaves that will be a dilemma of great consequence, " argued back the gentleman as his alcohol laden breath washed over William.

"Everyone is free to their own thoughts and persuasion Sir. If anything I would think Tennessee would be neutral," said William as he excused himself to attend to the other guests. The celebration continued well into the evening without any further problem with the unruly businessman. Finally the last guest left and William and Margaret were standing alone by the door. They stood in a long embrace until Elizabeth came and stood beside them. "It was a wonderful party," she said as she put her arms around both of them. "Everyone complimented on the beautifully dress you made for me Mother. I have the very best Mother and Father in the whole world. Thank you Daddy," she added as she kissed him on the cheek. In public she had always called him Father but in private moments she always used Daddy.

Sunshine called from the kitchen and said she would clean up in the morning.

Later in their bedroom upstairs William and Margaret slept in the same bed, unlike most people who chose to sleep separately. As Margaret blew out the kerosene lamp by their bedside she put her arm across his chest and whispered, "I love you."

The sound of a gunshot woke him up from a sound sleep. He immediately rose up in bed and listened. No other sounds or gunshots did he hear to tell him anything. His curiosity fully aroused he slipped the covers back and as he sat at the edge of the bed putting on his night slippers and robe against the early morning chill he assured himself it was a gunshot that had woke him up and not his imagination. Shivering slightly he went down the long staircase to the front vestibule. The hinges were well oiled and made no sound as he opened the front door. As he stood there in the chilled early light of morning he looked out into a dense fog that had came in overnight. A stray breeze caused the fog to swirl around him there was no sound.

As he tried to look through the thick blanket of mist he could just barely make out the front gate. There were people or rather shapes walking along the road. Against his better judgment he slowly walked towards the gate and as he got closer he could tell the shapes were soldiers and they were marching in unison but there was no sound. A chill ran up his spine! Standing by the gate he could see the shapes clearly. Rifles were slung over one shoulder and each rifle had a long bayonet attached. Then suddenly the soldiers disappeared as if the fog had enveloped them. Sunlight quickly shone through the fog and stung his eyes. He immediately brought his hand up to shield them against the glare. The scene in front of him changed and he was looking at two long lines of men and they were also soldiers.

Then as if in slow motion the two lines of soldiers brought their rifles up to their shoulders and as they fired a choking cloud of gun smoke obscured them from view. As he watched the soldier's guns fire there was no sound. The scene was eerie. William knew he had just witnessed dozens perhaps hundreds of men fire their weapons. The next scene to unfold was just as strange. It was early evening, almost sundown and he was standing alongside a line of cannons that stretched to his right for as far as he could see. Again a thick cloud swallowed him as the cannons belched fire and smoke. Behind the line of cannons William could see a white haired soldier wearing what looked like an officers uniform and he was sitting astride a magnificent horse. His posture was straight in the saddle and he was looking directly at William. As he stood there and watched a thick cloud of cold murky fog closed in around the soldier and he was gone.

As William looked around he was back inside the gate looking out into an impenetrable wall of thick vapor. The realization that he had just seen a vision hit him in hard in the stomach and had to grab hold of the wrought iron gate to keep from falling down. He had witnessed soldiers in the act of battle and killing each other. Up until that point he had remained neutral in his feelings about slavery but the upcoming war would be centered on the slavery issue and it would tear the country apart. In any war finances were at the center of everything and William knew in his heart he was only one man but possibly he could make a difference. He turned and walked back to the bedroom and tried to slip back into bed without waking Margaret but when she asked about the gunshot he just said it was some hunter getting an early start. Just before sleep overtook William he could not stop thinking about the piercing look the soldier on horseback had given him.

Chapter Thirteen

"Is something troubling you?" asked Margaret as they sat at the breakfast table.

"Wrong? No, I don't think so," answered William as he coughed and covered his mouth with a handkerchief.

"Something has been bothering you for almost two weeks and I don't mean the cough."

"Not much gets by you does it?" he said as he reached across the table to hold her hand.

"No, it doesn't and I will understand if you don't wish to talk about it."

"That's what I love about you. You are downright sneaky when you want to be," he said as he pushed away the half eaten breakfast plate of sausage, biscuits and gravy.

"Seriously, I am concerned is all. You haven't been yourself and seem to be in a daze most of the time."

"You remember the other night when the gunshot woke us up?"

"Yes, but you said it was just a hunter wanting to get an early start."

"In truth it probably was but when I went out to the front gate it was very foggy and as I stood there I am convinced I had a vision."

With the revelation of her husband having a vision she took her husband's hand in both of hers. She knew he was not a dreamer and subject to fanciful thoughts. "Tell me about it," she said, as she looked him in the eye.

"The fog was very thick that morning and as I watched a line of soldiers marched down the road. Then the scene changed to daylight and there were two long lines of soldiers standing and facing each other with rifles and they fired at each other. There were thick clouds of smoke and then the scene changed to late afternoon with a single long line of big field guns that fired continuously. Behind the line of cannons sat a white haired gentleman in uniform on a magnificent horse. He looked directly at me and then disappeared into the thick smoke from the guns. During the entire time not a sound was heard even while the cannons were firing."

He looked across the table at his wife fully expecting a look of scorn to be there but what he saw was one of admiration. "I have never told you this dear husband and I sincerely apologize but what you experienced was almost exactly in detail a dream I had the first evening on the General Jackson. I should have told you about it but I figured you would think it foolishness."

"In my vision," William continued, "I felt very strongly that I was to construct a huge vault under the plantation and to arrange for the transfer of large amounts of gold, silver and cash to be stored there to be used in support of a coming war over the slavery issue."

"Yes, I have felt for sometime the slavery issue was not a small one and would result in war. Sort of a woman's intuition."

"A few years ago I read an article in a newspaper somewhere and it commented on an English engineer by the name of John Cherry who had just finished a tunnel from some coalmines to the harbor thus saving a huge amount of time. I will send a letter to him and request his services and help to build the storeroom. I may have to be away for a few weeks to talk with a few banks willing to go along with the plan. Can you manage here while I am away?"

"Of course dear. Sunshine and I can manage just fine. The crops are already in and shipped to market. The fields plowed and seeds stored for next years harvest. The trip would be good for you anyway. You have been spending too much time in the mills and not allowing Mr. O'Malley to properly do his job as overseer."

What William did not tell his wife was that he had planned to go to England anyway to see a doctor who specialized in heart and lungs but didn't know how to justify the trip. His cough at the breakfast table had been occurring more frequently and during periods of long hours in the cotton mills he would have to stop and catch his breath.

It only took six weeks until a young man knocked on the front door. "Is this the residence of Mr. William Claibourne?" he asked. "I am John Cherry." "Yes," answered Sunshine as she took his hat and overcoat. "Please come in. I will get Mr. Clairbourne."

Margaret watched from the kitchen doorway as her husband and Mr. Cherry went into William's study and closed the door behind them. They did not come out until three hours had passed. William announced that Mr. Cherry would be joining them for dinner and would be a guest for several weeks perhaps months.

When John had received the letter requesting he come across the ocean to dig a root cellar with a connecting tunnel it sounded strange to say the least but the fee Mr. Claibourne quoted upon completion quickly erased any doubts and he arranged passage on the next ship. The next morning after a grand breakfast of sweet cakes, venison sausage, fruit, hot biscuits with white gravy and a delicious beverage made from crushed cocoa berries he rode into town to buy wood and heavy timbers that would be needed to shore up and support the tunnel walls and cellar from collapsing.

In their discussion Mr. Claibourne specifically mentioned the root cellar had to have cedar walls to help prevent worms and termites from invading and weakening the stanchions and support beams. For the tunnel Mr. Claibourne would trust his judgment on material types. He also stressed time was of the essence to have it completed for the spring garden some six months away. Mr. Cherry assured him it would be completed on time.

While Mr. Cherry was busy building the root cellar and tunnel William began building a small room in the upstairs attic to store any money that would be deposited by any banks before completion. From the banker in town he arranged to have a heavy wall safe delivered. Getting the heavy thing upstairs required a Herculean effort requiring a series of heavy-duty ropes and pulleys. To hide the safe from prying eyes William fashioned a large picture and thick frame to cover the metal edges of the safe. Inside the storeroom he cut out a stairwell in the center leading down to the bottom floor of the plantation directly over the underground vault and disguised the whole thing with a false wall. After Mr. Cherry had completed the vault he would cut an entranceway through the vault ceiling. John was curious about the construction in the plantation but knew it was none of his affairs besides the residents of Lindbergh had told him William tended to be a little eccentric at times.

Almost to the day four weeks later William was in his study finishing up a letter to a bank in Georgia to outline his proposal for storing funds in the underground vault when Mr. Cherry knocked on the door. "The root cellar and tunnel is finished Mr. Claibourne. It went surprisingly quick without any serious problems except the tunnel caved in twice. The water level in this area is very shallow and the tunnel floor is a scant eight feet above the table and extra shoring was required almost the entire length of the passageway. I base my name as an engineer on saying the tunnel and cellar are sound."

"Excellent work Mr. Cherry," said William as he put the letter in the drawer of his desk. "Please accept this bonus of a thousand dollars for completing the project ahead of schedule."

"You are most generous, Sir, but my original fee is quite sufficient. I will be returning to England in the morning."

"Then at least let me buy your ticket," insisted William.

"Agreed, Mr. Claibourne. It has been a pleasure to be a guest in your home and please extend my thanks to your wife. She is a marvelous cook."

Yes, I know all to well," responded William as he patted his stomach.

William breathed a sigh of relief as Mr. Cherry turned to leave his study. The vault was finished and just in time. The attic storeroom was becoming full at an alarming rate. It seemed many of the banks he had earlier contacted were already in the process of looking for suitable places to keep funds in strategic places in the event they had to be used quickly. It seemed the talk of war had the country all stirred up.

"Gentlemen, the war has been going badly for us," said General Lee as he stood in front of his officers. "We lost a lot of good soldiers at Gettysburg, almost 29,000 men and we can ill afford another defeat. Desertions are more frequent and moral is extremely low. I have sent word to General Hood in Tennessee and he will be joining us here in Virginia, perhaps in a month for an attack on Washington itself."

General Lee went on to explain the plan of attack on Franklin and then Nashville Tennessee by General Hood. At the center of the General's plan was a bold arrangement to use the funds being stored at Rosewood to buy guns, ammunition and food to support General Hood and have him bring the supplies with him to Virginia for the assault on the capitol. Before the battle for Gettysburg General Lee had made a secret visit to Rosewood and spoke with William about his plan. The General had traveled in civilian clothes in the event he might be seen but he also knew if he should be captured he could very well be shot as a spy before his identity could be revealed.

General Lee's plan to use the funds was fairly simple and that was to take the gold and silver only and leave the currency behind for another time. William explained to the General how much was stored in the vault, which was several millions in gold and silver coin, and ingots and the weight involved. "It can't be helped," said General Lee. "Both gold and silver are easily exchanged for supplies where currency is considered less desirable." "Yes, General I quite agree but the weight is my main concern and would require several heavy wagons at least to move the entire amount quickly and of course secrecy is utmost. Considering the amount of money involved I suggest only men that you trust implicitly."

"Excellent advice and sound reasoning," agreed General Lee. "One week from today I will arrange for three wagons to arrive here filled with wood and enough soldiers in civilian clothes to quickly transfer the wood to a place of your choosing and instructions on how much money to be loaded onto the wagons." "Agreed, General I shall begin immediately to fill as many strong boxes as possible and move them to the vault door for transfer."

The week passed quickly and just as General Lee had said the wagons arrived at the front gate late in the afternoon stacked high with cut wood and covered with canvas. The lead driver explained they were headed for Lindbergh to sell the wood for furs and take the furs to Nashville for trade. William offered the use of the barn for them to spend the night, as it was probably to late to do business in Lindbergh that day. Thanks were said and as the wagons rolled down the road a short way to the barn William silently wished them god speed and good luck then went back into the house.

"Margaret, I forgot to offer the gentlemen a cup of hot coffee. It is a little cold this evening and I am sure they would welcome something hot. I'll make a big pot and take some cups down to them in the barn." "That's nice dear," said Margaret, "And take some bear sign that Sunshine baked this morning with you." What William planned was not only to bring the men some hot coffee but also to open the underground vault door to allow them to transfer the gold and silver bullion to the wagons. The men were very happy to see William and the coffee pot but when they saw the bear sign covered in sugar it was almost like William had just brought them their discharge papers.

William explained the system he had made in the well house to go down into the well a short distance and into the tunnel then to the vault door. He would go first and open the door then go back to the house. Inside the vault he had stacked many strong boxes and attached a note as to the amount in each one so they wouldn't have to lose valuable time in counting. All that was required to lock the door was to close it behind then when they finished their business.

The distance from the vault door through the short tunnel was only thirty yards and William had made a very sturdy small four-wheeled wagon expressly for the purpose of moving the money to the well entrance. Kerosene lanterns were placed in regular intervals along the tunnel walls so there could be light. The soldiers divided into two teams of three each and worked quickly and efficiently. Their plan was to move the boxes from the vault and down the tunnel to the well entrance and from there the other three men would them up and put them in the wagons, place some of the wood over them and cover the whole thing with canvas to look as before. It was a good plan but what they had not counted on was the weight of the strong boxes.

It took all three of them to start the wagon rolling over the hard packed dirt tunnel floor toward the well entrance. One of the wagon wheels started squeaking loudly in protest and the sound was eerie in the small tunnel. Then the wheel stopped turning. "Okay, everyone behind the wagon and push," commanded the Lieutenant in charge. With everyone pushing the wheel started turning again but suddenly the wheel axel snapped into sending the wagon crashing into the tunnel wall. Even though the tunnel walls had been built strong and enforced overhead with solid oak beams they were no match for the weight of all the gold and silver stacked on the wagon, they collapsed, sending a massive amount of wood and dirt falling down onto the soldiers.

At the top of the well entrance the three soldiers saw the dust come out of the well and felt the rumble as the tunnel walls caved in. They immediately guessed what had happened and also knew it would be useless to try any kind of rescue. "Well, nothing to do now except try and get back to camp and tell what happened." As there were three of them each one climbed on a wagon and snapped the reins over the horses rumps and started out to where the army was camped thirty miles south of Franklin. It wasn't to be however because a union patrol spotted them and mistaking the covered wood for supplies shot and killed them.

General Hood was anxious to get started and felt his officers and men were not fighting their best because of Gettysburg. The much-needed supplies were a week overdue and General Lee had sent a messenger for him to meet him in Virginia as quick as possible. When he had crossed the Tennessee border he had commanded 40,000 men but after a failed meeting against General Schofield at Franklin he had lost some six thousand men.

Retreat was out of the question because a large part of his army was from Tennessee and that might cause some of them to want to stay. From somewhere a few reinforcements along with some cavalry straggled in and he decided to slowly advance toward Nashville hoping the over due and much needed supplies would get there in time.

Without the supplies General Hood's battle lines at Nashville were out flanked and pushed back. On December fifteenth, the next day Union forces renewed their attack and managed to get some cavalry forces around his left flank and combined with a frontal assault his entire left wing was routed. Without the support of the supplies he had lost some 15,000 men and was forced to retreat to Tupelo Mississippi. Shortly afterward in Virginia General Lee learned that Hood had resigned his command.

The next morning after William had taken the hot coffee and bear sign to the soldiers he went downstairs and seeing the wagons were not at the barn decided they had finished their business and left. Then he immediately sent word to the banks to stop sending money. As the vault had served its purpose he did not go into it again.

William's reputation as a solid and reputable citizen was well known among southern banks so there was no question of his honesty. The only thing troubling him was what excuse could he use to explain the trip to England to see the doctor without arousing her suspicions? The answer to his dilemma came in the morning mail the next day.

"Margaret would you pack a few things for me?" William called to his wife in the kitchen as he sat behind his desk in the study, "I have to go to England to settle an estate for an old friend. You remember Nathan Guilderhouse?"

"Yes, but not very well I am afraid. Wasn't he one of the guests at our reception?"

"Indeed he was. It seems he and his father were killed in an accident and a banker that handled their assets sent a letter saying I am the executor of his will. It sounds rather strange that he chose me but would you mind terribly if I went alone and took care of the matter?"

"Of course not dear. I have no desire to stay in a musty ship cabin for several weeks and besides being seasick is not very amusing especially if you happen to be the only female among a crew of sailors. Someday I am sure there will be women who sail on ships other than as passengers but I am just as sure it will not happen in my lifetime. Besides you love the ocean and the salt air will do you a world of good."

William wished going to England was for pleasure and not because of the death of an old friend and to see a specialist but it couldn't be helped. Sam had the buggy ready and waiting at the front gate to drive him to Lindbergh and catch the train to Nashville.

"Mistuh William you be leavin us fo a time?" asked Sam as he sat on the buggy seat and flicked the reins over the horses rumps to start them out.

"English please Samson" responded William.

"My apologies Mr. Claibourne. The habit of speaking broken English around people seems to be a hard one to break."

"I understand completely. Samson I will be away in England for several weeks to see a specialist but do not tell Mrs. Claibourne the nature of my trip only that I confided in you about the death of a good friend."

"The specialist is for your cough, Sir"

"He is and I have a feeling he will tell me it is not good. Remember the paper I wrote to explain you belonged to me in case any authorities should ask?"

"Yes Sir."

"I have it with me. Even though you never belonged to me officially and I thoroughly appreciate all the hard work you have done all these years. I want to thank you." As William handed Samson the letter he also handed him a heavy leather bag full of gold coins. "This is for your family," he explained. In town William and Samson shook hands as he boarded the train and as William sat down in the train seat he leaned back and closed his eyes. He did not feel comfortable about seeing the specialist at all. Perhaps Margaret was right about the sea air being good for him.

Chapter Fourteen

William leaned against the ship's rail and watched the slow roll of the ocean waves as they moved across the distant horizon. Memories flashed through his thoughts; thoughts of Margaret, Elizabeth and Rosewood. Memories of his youth and many days spent sitting patiently listening to university instructors as they lectured on business, memories of his father who had been a stern taskmaster in always expecting only the best from his only son, William. His father had seen that he attended only the finest universities in Europe where he learned the fine principles of running a business and his father had also expounded at great length a man was only as good as his word and to finish whatever he started. He also remembered the diagnosis given to him by the physician in London just three days earlier; that of Brown Lung disease.

Acting on the advice of his personal doctor, William had paid a visit to a much younger physician, a specialist in diseases of the lungs and heart who had earned a reputation in diagnosing such ailments and rarely was his judgment in error. Brown Lung disease, as he had advised William, was acquired by long hours spent in hot, sweltering cotton mills without proper ventilation. It had no known cure but a temporary amount of comfort could be realized by getting away from the mills and into clean air. The disease was nearly always fatal once diagnosed. He had given

William two years, three at the very most as his illness was in an advanced stage. William debarked the ship in Boston and from there bought passage on a train to Nashville and to home, Rosewood.

Discipline was a word the Sergeant knew but did not favor, as he much preferred robbing, looting and killing. The Captain had impressed upon him, earlier that week, the importance and urgency of their patrol. They were to scout the territory in advance of the regiments move on Nashville in ten days and under no circumstance were they to engage any Confederate units as that would give away their presence, alert the enemy and the element of surprise would be lost.

As a First Sergeant he had often led a squad or platoon of soldiers and as a Master Sergeant he had been in charge of a company but now he felt it was an insult to lead just three troops who were slovenly and miserable excuses for soldiers at best. Five days ago they had set out after provisioning for a ten-day patrol. The Captain had advised them to disguise themselves as they saw fit. They chose a mix of dirty and torn clothing to resemble poor and out of work cowmen. Against the advice of the Captain some had also chosen to wear short swords and heavy highwaymen pistols, common with renegades and outlaws.

For five days through dense forest undergrowth they had crawled and slogged through waist deep swamp only stopping long enough to eat a little food, often cold and eaten hurriedly. Time was of the essence. Mosquitoes and leeches plagued them unmercifully all of which caused the First Sergeant to regret volunteering for the mission and with each passing minute his mood grew fouler. He was angry and needed action. It was early morning as they lay in concealment along the roadside while a Confederate patrol of about a dozen soldiers passed by. It was then he remembered a plantation they had passed just after sunrise that morning. They had enough supplies to last the remainder of the patrol but it was not food that was on his mind. The plantation was ripe for picking.

It was Sunday morning and her parents had just left to go into town and attend church. In the stable Elizabeth quickly changed into the old blouse and man's pants she kept hidden in a secret place. She was going riding. Her father had caught her one time putting his saddle on the Morgan before she changed clothes and said they would be taking the carriage instead of each riding their own horses to town. The week before he had bought a bay mare for her. Elizabeth supposed he guessed she had been riding the Morgan because he said," Little girls should ride bay mares." "Really father," she responded," I'm a grown lady now at seventeen." Yes, but in my mind you are still the little girl that used to sleep in my arms." Elizabeth smiled as she remembered those times years ago when she would find her father sitting in the old rocker on the balcony in the late afternoon and she would sit in his lap and quickly fall asleep.

William did not push the issue of religion with his family as he figured everyone should choose their own road to travel so he did not question the reason Elizabeth chose to not go with them to Sunday church. As a child she had asked what happened to people when they died? Did they go to heaven right away? He had done his best to explain the belief held by many folks about salvation but said the choice was hers and did not press the issue any further.

She thrilled in her ride as she sat astride the big red Morgan stud like a man instead of sidesaddle like a woman. As she felt her mount's powerful muscles beneath her stretch out into a full gallop she leaned far forward over his neck and whispered, "Go, big boy, go!" Immediately she felt his strides lengthen even more and Elizabeth tightened the grip she had with her knees and let out the reins in her hands just a little more. She did not care if her hair would be a mess to comb later and she did not care if she would smell of sweat and horse lather when she finished the ride. Today she could be the son her father secretly wanted and not the prim and proper lady her mother tried so hard to coach her into being.

The miles quickly sped by as the two of them reveled in their ride that morning. Elizabeth lost herself in thought as the wind rushed through her hair. She remembered days past when her father would come in from the field, smelling of sweat and cotton dust and as was his custom, he would give each of them a huge hug and get scolded by her mother to go bathe before supper. At the beginning of each day, after a hearty breakfast, right before leaving to do the day's work, he would embrace each of them and say he loved them very much. She didn't mind if he would smell like a man after a day of work. He was her father.

The big Morgan had slowed to a stop and she wondered to what had alerted him. She leaned over his neck to rub the powerful muscles as she looked around through the dense woods. She was well hidden in the thick forest as she sat quietly rubbing her mount's neck to help calm him down after their hard ride then she heard voices. Through the woods ahead she could just barely see four horsemen as they cautiously made their way through the trees, not making a sound. She watched in concealment as they walked their mounts. Each carried a sword and as they walked they held one hand along their side to keep the weapon from making any noise of metal against metal. They did not act like town people or look like cow men because of the swords. Soldiers!

Elizabeth sat very still and silently prayed her mount would not make any noise to alert the horsemen to her presence. She waited until she was absolutely sure they were gone and out of earshot and then she quickly urged the big Morgan once again into a full gallop, she had to get back to the plantation and inform her father of their presence. The woods surrounding Rosewood were very familiar to Elizabeth and she knew several shortcuts through the forest to get back home. She knew exactly where she was even though she had allowed the Morgan to chose the route for their ride that morning. Arriving back at Rosewood she quickly bathed away the evidence of her ride and changed into the clothes of a young lady. She just barely managed to quickly run to the stable and hide the riding clothes in their special place and get back into the house when she heard the sound of horses in the front of the house. It was not customary for horses to be in front of the plantation. They were supposed to be kept in the stable. Quickly she decided to hide in her secret place underneath the stairwell.

Inside her special hiding place Elizabeth sat in the darkness as she heard the men bang on the front door instead of knocking like gentlemen. She did not move as the sound of footsteps came through the thin wall of her concealment.

Elizabeth had played the hiding game many times as a small girl and she knew all the good places in the old house, except now it was not a game and she was hiding in fear for her life. She could hear the men as they shouted and cursed while going from room to room in search of anything of value to steal. She tried to be very quiet. She carefully put her ear to the thin wall of the door where she was hiding. It was just a small, old storage place beneath the staircase and only had one; small opening that would slide like a pocket door into the wall. It appeared to be a very tiny space since the wall behind her also would slide open to enter the passages that went through the house. It even had a tiny staircase that lead to the second floor. She had often played the game when mother needed her to do some small chore or wanted her to sit quietly while she told her about how a 'proper' young lady should act in the presence of a gentleman, be courteous and no tomfoolery. She tried her best to be patient with her Mother whenever she would talk to her about being a lady.

Elizabeth Anne Claiborne, a fine young lady of seventeen and of old southern family traditions, and lately of Rosewood Plantation in Tennessee, but her family roots originated in Atlanta Georgia. Her mother and father were not sympathetic to the slavery issue, which was threatening to bring civil war to the nation and was the reason for them moving from Atlanta in 1846. Papa, as she lovingly called her father, liked fine furniture, so when they moved from Atlanta he had all their furnishings moved with them. He had made a deal with a Judge Henry of New York who had a set of French bedroom furniture carved from rosewood. After delivery of the furniture, he liked the color and texture of the wood so much that he had the entire house furnishings made from rosewood, so naturally he named the plantation Rosewood. The year was 1864 and they had found a peaceful place of refuge here eighteen years ago and had started a business of growing and shipping cotton to the eastern markets, when war between the North and South brought chaos to their lives. Bands of rebels would often ride by the plantation, shooting and shouting, none of them had stopped, however, until now.

The men cursed as they stomped and ran through the old plantation. Elizabeth sat very quiet and prayed her hiding place would be good enough again as it had before. She could hear the men coming down the staircase from the bedrooms upstairs. Their loud, vulgar words upset her, as she had never heard such foul language. She was very frightened. Where was Charles she wondered? He often came by the plantation on the way to his house. He always used the excuse of asking if he could water his horse but she knew he secretly liked her. They had not talked of marriage, but young ladies knew of such things long before the idea had even occurred to fine eligible bachelors like Charles.

Charles Edwin Berringer was a fine young man of twenty summers and came from a family of English land barons who had moved to the colonies to start a winery and ship to the western frontier towns that were growing bigger and more rowdy by the day. While riding one day he had seen Elizabeth as she walked in the garden by the front porch of Rosewood and immediately decided he would one day ask her to marry him.

Elizabeth held her breath as the foul men came down the stairs. A cramp was beginning to form in her legs from being crouched up in such a small place for so long. She could hear their footsteps as they walked across the wooden floor and stopped right outside her hiding place. The cramp was hurting very much so she tried to relax one leg and accidentally bumped the wall of her hiding place. Suddenly one of the men yanked open the small door and roughly pulled her out into the area between the entry and the sitting room. She tried to appear small and helpless so as not to offend them.

Elizabeth evaluated her situation. Here she was alone and surrounded by soldiers. She could not tell exactly which side they were from, North or South, as their clothes were so dirty and torn. Two of the soldiers were carrying one of her mother's chests. Without thinking she shouted,

"Put that down, that belongs to my mother!"

Startled by the tone of her voice one of the soldiers dropped his end of the chest. This outraged Elizabeth even more.

"What do you mean coming into my parent's house and stealing our things?" She asked indignantly.

"Why ma-am, you have plenty to go around for everyone here," said the soldier who was still holding his end of the chest as he looked brazenly at Elizabeth's body.

Then the other soldiers looked at each other as their coarse laughter rang menacingly through the hallway. Trying to contain her anger, Elizabeth said, "You men are filth, when my father comes home he will deal with you severely."

"What is all this shouting about?" asked another soldier as he was coming down the staircase.

"Sergeant, this here girl is telling us her father will give us trouble when he gets home," said one of the soldiers as he laughed.

Muttering curses under his breath, the soldier came down the staircase the rest of the way. "This girl is ordering you around like common house slaves. You are miserable excuses for soldiers. Tie her up. She will go with us."

"I will do no such thing," said Elizabeth, indignantly. "This is my father's house and you men need to leave, or I will…"

"You will what?" snarled the sergeant. He stood very close to Elizabeth.

She quickly brought her scented handkerchief up to her nose to hide the foul odor of the man. He needed a bath.

"Bring her with us," commanded the Sergeant.

"Uh, Sarge, do you think it is a good idea to take her with us, seeing as how we still have that job the Captain gave us to do?"

"Hmmm, yes, you are right," said the Sergeant. "She would be a bother, but we can hardly leave her here to tell other folks we were here, now can we?"

"Oh please, if you will just leave, I will not say a word about you even being here, you have my word, sir. Will you just kindly leave?"

"No," said the Sergeant, "That would not work, we have already torn up some furniture and you would not be able to explain that to your father to his liking, you will go with us."

Elizabeth quickly gathered her dress and bolted for the front door! One of the soldiers reached out and grabbed her by the arm as she ran past him.

She looked at each soldier. "Please, you can have anything in the house and if you ask my father I am sure he will give you what ever you need to continue your journey," said Elizabeth as pleadingly as she could.

"Please?" she asked the Sergeant. "You seem to have a few more manners than the others, will you take your men and what ever you can carry and leave?'

"Well, missy, it seems as if I have left my manners at home," said the Sergeant as he was looking over Elizabeth's body.

Suddenly he reached out and grabbed the top of Elizabeth's dress. The lace and fine chiffon came away in his hand revealing her fine lace underclothes. The soldiers crowded around her, their hands pulling and hurting as they ripped away her under things. They each tried to push and shove each other away. Their body odors and foul breath caused Elizabeth to faint. Their harsh and cruel laughter rang out through the hallways of the house as they pulled at Elizabeth's half-clothed body.

Her innocent blood stained the wooden floor as the soldiers savagely assaulted her unconscious body. At some time during the following hour she mercifully died.

Chapter Fifteen

Today was the day, Charles decided, that he would stop at Rosewood Plantation. He was dressed in his best riding clothes, a black short-waisted jacket, tan cap, brown riding trousers and black polished, calf length riding boots, all custom made for him by a private tailor. Of course, it would be on the pretense of watering his horse as in the past few times he had rode by. If that fine young lady was about, then he would ask permission of her father if he might marry his daughter as she had surely stolen his heart.

Charles had guessed her to be about seventeen possibly eighteen and her beauty was beyond words. He had often seen her walking in the garden, and such a beautiful garden it was too, and he wanted to stop and chat so dearly, but they have not yet been formally introduced, so any lengthy conversation was absolutely out of the question. He had waved to her as he rode past the Plantation and she had waved back, twice he had waved and each time she would take her handkerchief and slowly wave it back and forth. Could a man endure such exquisite pain and live he wondered?

As he rode down the long dusty road, he rehearsed his proposal. He reasoned that she liked him at least a little, after all, she had waved back to him, twice, and if she were not interested in him, she would have ignored him altogether. He rounded the last turn in the road before the plantation. He could see several horses tied at the rail by the front porch. This was not as it should be, he decided. Usually, horses weren't tied at the rail; a houseboy always took them away to the stable. He counted four horses, and they were in need of proper care. They had not been curried and combed in sometime and their tack was in sad disorder. Immediately he was suspicious. He looked for the young lady, but she was not to be seen. He had heard reports of roving bands of rebels and vandals in the area. He did not have an invitation to step down from his horse but he felt it would be acceptable in this instance, so he rode his horse up to the rail and taking the rains in one hand, he dismounted and tied his horse at the rail.

He had reached the first step of the porch when the wooden front door slammed open. He stood there looking at four men, unshaven, dirty and unkempt clothing, two were wearing short swords and one had a heavy highwayman's pistol stuck in the waistband of his trousers. They were a troublesome looking group. It was not his place to challenge them as it was not his house but he felt it was proper in this case.

"Can I help you gentlemen with anything?" he asked?

His calling them gentlemen caused the soldiers to laugh loudly. "Gentlemen?" They laughed again.

"Now that is something, calling us gentlemen," said one of the men.

Charles decided to try another way. "Perhaps you would care to rest your horses in the stable and I am sure there is food in the house for you to take on your journey."

"Oh, we have already been in the house," said the soldier who had the pistol in his waistband. "Yeah," answered the others as they began to laugh and poke each other with their elbows.

Immediately Charles decided that something was very wrong. "Then if you gentlemen have no further business here you can leave." His voice was firm as his hand came up to rest on the handle of his sword.

"Now look at that," said one of the soldiers, "he wants to challenge us."

The soldiers drew their short swords and slowly began to circle around him. Charles drew his saber, a fine, lightweight weapon and easily controlled. His father had been an excellent champion swordsman and had taught Charles a few skills with many types of weapons. With his left hand, he drew a two-shot derringer from within his jacket. He quickly fired and struck one man in the left side of his chest. He hurriedly fired again but this time only grazing another man on the arm. He flung the derringer at them and advanced with his sword flashing in short cuts back and forth. He quickly dispatched one man with a parry and a slash to his sword arm, then a cut deep into his middle. One of the other soldiers was on his left side, so he quickly took two steps and was within range. One slash and the soldier crumpled into a heap on the porch floor, his blood pooling underneath his body.

Youth and stamina were his advantage against the two remaining soldiers. His arm was strong from many hours of practice as he wielded his blade in a wall of steel style of fighting. His sword flashed in the morning sunlight as he forced the two swordsmen down off the porch and into the yard to give him a little more room to work. A faint smile was upon his lips as he reveled in the challenge even though it was no sport but a game of death.

His weapon of choice was a custom made European dueling sword with qualities of a Confederate foot soldiers weapon with an extra two inches added to its standard length of twenty-eight inches. In any fight the extra length was a decided advantage. The blade's composition was of a carbon steel alloy, very flexible without the curve of a standard saber and the total weight was slightly less than two pounds; a formidable weapon in the right hands.

In the days of pirates and buccaneers sword fights were usually done using heavy cutlasses with flat blades and in the style of exaggerated overhead and side slashes requiring an enormous amount of strength. The swords of choice later became the rapier and the epee or dueling sword with weight and flexibility being the main concern and instead of large movements of the arm a style of adroitness and skill using mostly the point and last few inches of the weapon or parry and riposte.

With a deft skillful move Charles drove his sword point deep into the sword arm at the shoulder of one soldier rendering him useless. He turned his full attention to the remaining soldier his confidence was high. Suddenly the Sergeant flicked his weapon and drew blood from Charles's chest, right above his heart. It wasn't a serious cut, just enough to suggest his skill was equal to the task. He quickly raised his sword in an engarde position in front of his body signifying he had formal training and was silently informing his opponent, *prepare to defend yourself Sir.* Charles immediately realized he was in the fight of his life

For the better part of a half hour the noise of steel upon steel rang through the morning air as neither swordsman could achieve an advantage and give the other a serious wound. Each was of the same approximate age and each was in excellent health and their skills were equally matched. Each had chosen the style of parry and riposte even though the Sergeant's weapon was a standard Calvary saber and a little heavy for the style.

Charles adroitly lunged then parried with an overhead move then lunged again but this time with a slight lift of his wrist he drew blood on his adversary's sword shoulder. It was not a serious cut but if unattended the loss of blood could quickly weaken the stamina of one's opponent. The Sergeant realized he had made a mistake and adopted the style used by pirates of exaggerated, cut and slash movements. Charles was amazed at the strength of his foe considering the length of time they had already been fighting. Drawing on an inner reserve of stamina he withstood the furious attack and only his skill with his blade saved himself from death.

A movement in the corner of his eye caused Charles to quickly look to his right. During the heat of battle he had forgotten about the soldier he had wounded in the shoulder, a deadly mistake. The wounded soldier had crawled to one of the fallen soldiers and now lay on his side along the edge of the porch steps, he had a heavy highwayman's pistol in his hand and he fired. The large bullet struck Charles in the stomach right above his waistline, which caused him to fall to one knee from the impact. With a supreme effort Charles rose to his feet to finish the fight, he was shot again. Throwing caution to the wind he advanced upon the Sergeant, determined that if he must die then it would be a grand finish.

Reverend Johnson looked up from his prepared notes for his sermon that morning. It was Easter Sunday and he was expecting a full house. The townspeople were diligent in attending church as most country folk were but Easter and Christmas were special days. The night before had been spent in prayer.

He had not been called to be a preacher very long, only about five years but recently and more each day it seemed, he would feel a pressing need for prayer. Often he would know whom the prayer was for but more often he would not. However, last night he knew exactly who the prayer had been for; Mr. Claybourne. As he looked out over the congregation that morning he could see that everyone was in attendance with the exception of Elizabeth, William's daughter. He had seen her occasionally when she would come into town with her father, usually Saturday, when he would do some business with the local men. On one of those occasions she had stopped to chat as he was preparing some ground in front of the church to plant some flower seeds. She had been to Mendelson's, the town's general store and came out carrying a parcel underneath her arm. Without being intrusive he had noticed a small piece of fabric sticking out from the packaging. White lace and brocade. Wedding dress material, he wondered?

Two years ago he had arrived at Lindbergh after he had heard the sad news the town's minister had passed away. The church building was of good size and had been kept up very well so there wouldn't be much preparation to moving in. In a small room to the side of the pulpit he found a small roll top desk used by many pastors to keep baptismal, birth, marriage and death records. As he was looking through the files he found a note attached to the birth record of Elizabeth Claybourne. As he read the carefully written message he understood why Elizabeth did not attend church with her family.

The note was from the previous pastor. When Elizabeth was five years old she had came to services one Sunday and stood with her parents as they waited their turn in line to greet him and shake hands as was customary for the congregation to do. When it cane her turn he leaned down to shake her small hand and she had whispered if little girls went to heaven when they died like her father had said? It seemed a little irregular but he said to come and visit him at church the next, time her father came into town on business. During that conversation she had asked about her father telling her about salvation and could little girls go to heaven like that? He was an old man and well into the last years of his ministry but he had never heard of anyone ask so innocently about salvation. Together the two of them sat in a pew and talked. He had to wipe the tears away several times during their conversation.

It was shaping up to be a fine day, thought William, as he sat on the seat of the carriage. He and Margaret, his wife, were just coming home from church in town and he was thinking of how they had emigrated from France twenty years before. From the small villages and limited means of making any money at Portsmouth, they had moved to Atlanta but their sympathies did not agree with the local people who were Southerners, and the slavery issue, so they had moved to Tennessee where they had found rich farmland. There they had started their own mills and soon were shipping cotton to the markets in the east. Tennessee had not yet declared which side to join at first but as time went along it was clear they favored the south. William had a fine, beautiful wife and she had given him a precious daughter seventeen years ago but because of complications at childbirth, she was unable to have any others. He loved his family more than life itself.

In church that morning the congregation had sung all the verses of "Shall We Gather at the River", when they normally only sang two. He hummed the tune as he, with one hand, flicked the reins across the rump of the two horses pulling the buggy, and he softly held Margaret's hand with his other one. He recalled it seemed a little strange that morning when Mr. Johnson shook his hand after services. He had looked directly into his eyes and said discreetly, "Go home quickly!"

Yes indeed, it was going to be a fine day, thought William. The small country town and church with its white washed sides was soon left behind, in the clouds of dust stirred up by the horses and buggy. Very soon, the brown dust gave way to the lush green grasses and colorful flowers that surrounded Rosewood. William had promised himself that someday he would have a plantation, when he found the right place, and it would be the finest in the country. It would have deep carpets of green grass and thousands of varieties of flowers from all over the country, especially roses.

Rosewood looked a little out of place among the dusty roads and dry, brown countryside, with its tall columns of white Birchwood supporting the second and third decks in the front of the plantation but it was their home and that was all that was important. He helped Margaret down at the front porch and then he led the team to the barn. At the stable, he watered the horses and was just getting the comb and brush to rub them down when a terrified scream come from the house. Dropping everything, he ran to the front steps of the house and took them in two strides.

There in the front entranceway by the bottom of the staircase he saw Margaret sitting on the floor, her arms curled around Elizabeth's bare shoulders. Elizabeth's eyes were closed as her head lay heavily against her mother's breast. Margaret had partially covered Elizabeth's body with some of her torn clothing and was crooning softly as she rocked back and forth, as she had done so many times when Elizabeth was a baby. William took in the scene in one glance; the broken and turned over furniture, the torn clothing scattered about the room and the bloodstains on the floor by the small door of the stairwell. He felt a deep emptiness in his chest. He knelt there beside his wife and daughter and wept bitter tears as he put his arms around both of them.

Chapter Sixteen

As William knelt on the floor holding his family he would appear to be a broken man. He wept profusely but slowly a thundering rage began building in his heart. Rising up from the floor, he went back outside. In his haste to be with Margaret, he had overlooked some dark stains on the front porch. He looked more closely now and read what he saw like a map the scrape marks from muddy boots, the blood spots in two places, the now empty derringer and more scrape marks leading down the steps toward the garden. He followed the drag marks on the ground and as he looked further ahead, he saw a figure tied to the willow tree in the back of the garden. Looking at the ground, he could see that a terrific fight had taken place here. He recognized the figure of the young man as the same one who often rode by on his horse as Elizabeth was walking in the garden. In an instant, he guessed the details and went to see if the young man was still alive.

As he neared the willow tree, he took in the cut of the clothes, the well-polished boots, the tailored riding clothes and the fine features of the young man. He guessed him to be about twenty and well dressed, the horse he had been riding was a beautiful well-bred black stallion. The tack on the horse cost more than just a few dollars. The young man had been shot twice and was then allowed to bleed slowly to death there on the tree after his torturers had taken their turns with their knives on his chest and arms. His jacket and shirt had been ripped to shreds and was pulled back as they had done their dirty work. His broken sword lay at his feet. He had died gallantly defending his daughter's honor. William knew the young man's family and he would return their son to them as soon as he made sure that Margaret and Elizabeth were cared for. William noticed also in addition to the blood obliviously from the young man there were several spots of blood, leading away from the tree, as if the attackers were wounded themselves and bleeding.

After William had taken Charles's body to his parent's home, he slowly road back to Rosewood. Looking at the beautiful Magnola trees and listening to the birds singing he looked toward the sky and closed his eyes and murmured, "Oh! Lord how could such a terrible thing happen to those I love on such a beautiful day?" There he vowed to make the plantation garden a living memorial to Elizabeth and the young gentleman. He would spare no expense but first he would track down the pair of men that had so brutally taken the life of his daughter and young Charles.

In the stable he saddled the big red mare and mentally prepared himself for a long journey, if necessary. He packed some jerky and hard biscuits and water. A wave of sadness overcame him as the memory of Elizabeth lying in his wife's arms flashed through his thoughts. The memory served to harden his resolve. They would pay and pay dearly for their mistake. As William sat on his in the front yard the tracks were easy to pick up as the men had been in a great hurry to leave. He urged his mount forward into an easy trot as he followed the tracks out of the yard and into the woods that surrounded Rosewood on three sides.

As William followed the easy trail it was evident the men were either drunk or wounded as the tracks stopped many times apparently to change their bandages they had made from torn up rags or shirts. The anger continued to build and rose up in his heart. His horse stamped in impatience to be off and moving. After only about six miles of tracking William stopped at the edge of a small meadow and quietly dismounted. He could see across the way that the two had stopped to rest. Vengeance rose up in William's heart as he took his rifle from the saddle boot. He would end it here and he would end it now. Throwing caution to the wind he swiftly ran across the meadow fully expecting the two men to get up and either protect themselves or try to run away like cowards. They did neither.

William stood over the two men, as they lay dead on the forest ground. He studied their bodies. Young Charles had represented himself exceedingly well in defending his daughter's honor. The dead men bore many cuts to their upper body and it was amazing they had ridden as far as they had before succumbing to their wounds. William knew it was the Christian thing to give the two a decent burial but chose to leave them where they lay to rot on the forest floor. He gathered the reins of the men's horses, mounted his own mare and returned to Rosewood. There he made plans to build the memorial garden.

The small town of Lindbergh just down the road from Rosewood had few conveniences of a larger city but it had the one thing that William needed very badly, a telegraph office. Over the next two days, William sent telegrams to most of the major towns and cities around the state. The telegrams stated that there was work to be had at Rosewood plantation. Work for masons, millwrights, iron workers and field hands. Very soon, after the word went out heavy wagons began arriving at Rosewood. Wagons of lumber, slabs of quarry stone, small trees ready for planting and dozens of skilled workers, ready to build whatever needed. The last to arrive was an elderly oriental gentleman from the east. He inquired of William if there was work there for him also. William was doubtful but asked if he knew of working with marble rock.

"Yes, I have such knowledge, Sir. What is it you wish to build?"

"What I had in mind was a bridge spanning a small stream in the back of the garden, about fifteen feet long and about eight feet wide. Can you do it?"

"Yes, it can be done. I have longed for years to build one in the likeness of a pagoda, would this be agreeable, sir?

A *pagoda*? William wondered. Well, why not, he had liked the far eastern countries anyway and he knew Elizabeth would also love it. "What payment would you require?" he asked of the gentleman.

"The stone is already here so payment would be only for my time and skill. It would be complete in sixty days; would $200 be too much?"

"$200 it is then, I shall look forward to seeing it."

William decided the garden would be in three sections; each would be unique in its own design. There was much work to be finished. In the months to follow, the townspeople of Lindbergh watched as the wagons continued to roll down the road to Rosewood and they saw the columns of smoky haze rising from the cook fires, needed to feed the dozens of workers and field hands, and from the furnaces of the millwrights and iron workers. Everyday some of the ladies from town would come with cornbread and biscuits and sweet rolls. They wanted to help out in what way they could. William would often take time from his demanding schedule of keeping the mills running full-time and sit in a comfortable chair on the back porch of Rosewood to watch as the skilled artisans plied their trade. Soon massive walls on two sides began to take shape.

A maze of stone-piping waterways, fed from an artesian well, wound through the garden to water the plants and to keep the many small ponds full. In the ponds were very small islands of stones, evergreen shrubs and earth. The warm brown of summer turned into the panoramic reds and golds of fall. Later William would get some koi and other decorative fish for the ponds. The chilled morning air brought soft colorful morning clouds followed by the warm morning sun. William was very generous with paying the artisans their regular wages. The work was long and hard. He would often give outdoor parties for just the men and their families. Long tables would be set up, each filled with meat, vegetables and deserts. There would be dancing to fiddles, flutes and drums. Then after three years, the workers left and the cook fires were extinguished. Each of the artisans vowed to return, or their son's would, every so often to maintain the garden, as a token of William's generosity. It was late summer. The work was finished.

Rosewood garden was enclosed on two sides with tall hedges of boxwood and solid walls of mortared stone. It had two vantage points where the entire garden could be seen while sitting in a comfortable chair. One point was here on the back porch of Rosewood and the other was from the guesthouse in the rear right corner. The garden was modeled after the walled gardens of the middle ages when gardens of this style were said to symbolize freedom and beauty with its precisely set boundaries of hedges and rock walls would later be covered with vines of Jasmine and Honeysuckle and also Forsythias.

The garden was organized into individual areas, each of which had its own unique style and color plan. Throughout the garden wound a small-stone pathway, barely three feet wide made from crushed granite. Many of the rooms were almost enclosed with greenery from shrubs and flowers of profuse colors. William's knowledge of plants was extensive. He selected a great number of evergreen shrubs, flowers and plants from around the world. His favorites were of course roses but he also enjoyed, azaleas, rhododendrons, red blooming dogwoods, which often grew to over fifteen feet. There would be only three tall trees in the garden; one was a Japanese flowering cherry tree. It would grow to be about thirty feet tall. It was a gift from the oriental gentleman and occupied the rear of the garden by the guesthouse. It was a weeping variety and its branches were already beginning to sweep the ground. Another was a tall, stately, red oak, which would grow to maybe ninety feet high, and the third was a scarlet oak, which stood by the low boxwood hedge along the roadway entrance and a single weeping willow tree.

William had read somewhere about the legend that its boughs first drooped under the weight of the harps, as the exiled Hebrews sang: "By the waters of Babylon we sat down and wept when we remembered thee, O Sion! As for our harps, we hanged them up upon the willow-trees that are therein." The Arabian storytellers, however, have a very different tale to tell. They relate that David, after he had married Bathsheba, was one day playing on his harp in his private chamber, when two angels appeared before him and convinced him of his sin. Thereupon he threw himself upon the ground, and lay forty days and forty nights weeping bitter tears of penitence; and in those forty days he wept as many tears as the whole human race have, or ever will, shed on account of their sins, from then until the Day of Judgment.

According to legend his weeping was so great two streams of tears flowed out into the garden, whence there sprang up two trees, the Weeping Willow with lily of the valley peeping up through the lush grass and the Frankincense-tree, the boughs of the one drooping in grief, whilst the other constantly distills tears of sorrow. With the help of the landscapers and gardeners, he planned the blooming sequence of all the plants in Rosewood, ensuring there would be color almost year round.

Throughout the garden stood perhaps a hundred works of wrought iron fashioned by the ironworkers with their hammers and furnaces. The gate by the roadway entrance was massive with its rustic patters of oak branches, twigs and leaves tied together with iron ropes. William had seen the style in an old publication put out by a gentleman some 50 years before. The book was by J.L Mott of New York, which favored the style of broad leaves, long stemmed flowers and morning glories for chairs and small outdoor furniture, and William decided that was the style he wanted for Rosewood.

He also knew that wrought iron needed to be oiled lightly every so often to prevent rusting but that could not be helped. In particular, William wanted a chair fashioned from wrought iron, four feet long, three feet wide with a high back and the legs had to resemble the curved forks of a tree with gnarled roots. The iron had to have the characteristic rounded outer edges and the sharp inner edges familiar to hand-worked iron. Most importantly, he wanted the chair put on a slab of white granite four inches thick. It was late summer but the garden promised a late season of color from the plan that William had designed. He decided to take a long walk, slowly through the garden, looking at every detail that the artisans had worked so hard to put together. He noticed a very large stag-horned buck drinking from one of the ponds and also a few ducks and geese and a pair of large white swans. What a beautiful sight he thought to himself a slight chill made his heart grow warm.

To his left was a huge, solid wall of stones, soon to be covered by honeysuckle vines with their fragrant purple and violet blooms. In the first room, he saw Old Pink Mosses and white Alba roses. As he walked he saw low bushes of roses; soft reds of Centifolias or cabbage roses as some folks liked to call them, their fragrances heavy with the late afternoon warmth. Here was also a single bush of white Comtesse de Murinais moss roses with their burrs of hair on their stems and small-undeveloped buds and an umbrella of wrought iron covered with large, white Blanche roses. The next room was filled with arbors covered with light pink Jeanne de Montfort and deep maroon, almost black, Nuits de Young roses. To offset the red colors a few bushes of yellow Safrano tea roses were also there.

The next room was a little different in style. It had several stone statues of children playing what looked like skip-rope surrounded by dense bushes of holly with small buds of red. Randomly spread out was a few small bushes of light pink Bon Silene roses. Their fragrance was usually strongest in the cooler months if the temperature does not fall below twenty degrees.

The next turn in the graveled walkway brought William to the rear of the garden where the stone pagoda sat over a small stream. It was designed in the oriental cup-style to honor the pagoda. He saw the oriental gentleman has done his work well. In addition to the pagoda, he had added some touches from his home country; carefully placed, symmetrical plantings including bamboo and katsurra trees, long leafy ferns and delicate iris and lilies are everywhere. There were also two freeform ponds, one on each side of the pagoda with the stream in the middle. As he stopped along the rock pathway he leaned over a small pond and watched the afternoon clouds reflected in the stillness of the water. Statuary including cranes to represent wisdom and long life stand beside carefully placed small stones and rocks to represent the earth's natural forms. There were several areas of raked sand to represent the oceans tides and waves. This was more commonly known as a sand garden. In the two ponds were a single small group of white stones, a tiny bonsai tree and smooth light brown sand. Overhead is the Japanese Cherry tree. It stood as if it is keeping sentinel over the bridge, its long graceful lines almost touching the ground as they slowly moved in the afternoon breeze. William looked more closely at the stones of the pagoda bridge; he could not see any mortar between the stones. He wondered how the old gentleman had secured the stones together.

In the rooms ahead William saw many more works of wrought iron; archways covered by red and yellow tea roses. Freestanding stanchions wound around with deep red Gloire des Rosomanes which some have given the name Ragged Robin, and tall well-manicured bushes of pink Hermosa Bourbon roses and creamy white teas of the Devoniensis variety. The last room William came to contained his favorite rose of the entire garden, a variety of Noisette, the Aimee Vibert. Vibert was one of the great early hybridists. He wanted to create a pure white Noisette.

William had heard of the gentleman and his efforts to create his rose. This was perfect for what William also wanted. He wanted a pure white rose to symbolize the innocence that had been so brutally taken away from Elizabeth and it had to be petite like Elizabeth and had to be hardy enough to withstand the cold winter, as she liked to take long sleigh rides in the snow. Most importantly, the rose had to have a unique fragrance. William had commissioned Mr. Vibert to perfect the rose the same year the garden was started and gave him a time frame of three years to complete the job. A stipulation of Mr. Vibert was the rose would bear his daughter's name, which William agreed to right away. Mr. Vibert presented William with the Aimee Vibert rose two years later.

The Aimee Vibert was very hardy and often still had blooms in the early winter while light snow was on the ground and it often flooded the garden late in the afternoon with its soft blanket of fragrance. It could have reached heights of ten feet or more if allowed to ramble freely, but here William kept it on an arbor of French Timber design made of wrought iron; in the center of the arbor stood the specially made chair on the granite slab. He sat down in the chair and looked out at the garden; he was well pleased but very sad. The garden and the upkeep of maintaining the plantation had exacted a very heavy toll. He had paid a visit to his doctor in Nashville the summer before and was told he had a terminal illness, called Brown Lung disease. His doctor also recommended that he get a second opinion from a young physician in Europe whose specialty were diseases of the heart and lungs.

His personal doctor was a good man, honest and straightforward with his many patients but he was also aware of his limitations of new technology and highly recommended that William go to Europe for consultation and get an expert opinion. William sighed heavily when the young doctor had confirmed the diagnosis of Brown Lung. It had no known cure but an amount of limited comfort could be realized by getting away from the hot, sweltering cotton mills and into clean air. He had given William only two more years, three at the most as the disease was always eventually fatal. As William sat in his favorite on the back porch, overlooking the garden watching the array of butterflies and several hummingbirds chase each other as he drifted off to sleep. He dreamed.

He dreamed of when he was a young man in the deep woods surrounding the University of Nottingham in England. He dreamed of many hours sitting back against an old oak tree and reading a favorite book. This place gave him a sense of solace and peace when he didn't have time to get to his other secret place. The canopy of trees overhead allowed very little sunlight to penetrate to the forest floor below. The woods were Williams' escape from the harsh rigors of education at Nottingham and from the stuffy world of being a businessman that his father tried so desperately to force upon him. Later in life he was thankful for the discipline instilled by his taskmaster father

William thoroughly enjoyed time spent in solitude among the forest creatures, squirrels, chipmunks and rabbits as they waited in the shadows to quickly dart out and snatch a choice morsel of food and then just as quickly scurry back into the shadows, invisible. He loved the scents of morning rain that had collected on the plant leaves and fragrant aromas of flowers that abounded throughout the forest.

He was not a hunter by nature but felt comfortable and very much at home in the woodland. Surely this was how the first male, Adam felt as he walked in the garden and made his first steps as a man.

Chapter Seventeen

Of late, William had acquired a fondness of sitting on the back porch in his favorite chair overlooking the garden and watching the craftsmen as they plied their trades. Margaret would at times find him sleeping in his chair. One such morning she found him. He looked at peace. He had quietly passed away during the night.

It was four thirty in the morning and Sam was bone tired as he lay on a simple mattress of dusty wool blankets and corn-shuck ticking. The rooster had already crowed once. It was Saturday and they did not normally work today but it was crop time, the cotton was ready and it had been a very good year. He was bone tired. His old body, now in his late sixties was simply wore out and he was tired in his spirit as well.

Alaye lay on the simple bed he and his wife Asesimba shared. He reflected back over the many years since he had heard the sound of his real name. Before he and his wife had come to America he had been chieftain of his tribe. He became chief when his father died from injuries he received on a lion hunt. His father had been mauled very badly and infection quickly set in from not having good medical care. Alaye enjoyed the life of royalty for many years but a younger brother challenged him for the right to be chief. In the long fight that followed his rival threw sand into his eyes after he allowed him to get up from under his spear point as he lay on the ground. Then it was a quick end to finding himself on the ground under a spear point.

His mistake was thinking his younger brother was a man of honor. After his loss of the fight for the right to rule he and his wife were banished from the tribe. Rather than face a life of shame and ridicule from the other tribes people they decided to come to the new Americas and start a new life. He and his wife still shared their native language in their private moments but in public they always spoke in broken English typical of black slaves.

Mr. William had named him Samson after he found out that he could lift one end of a cotton bale clear of the ground. Sometimes a full bale could weigh over four hundred pounds. Usually though everyone that knew him just called him Sam. Through the years a friendship had developed between Samson and William. Early after their first meeting years ago William had indeed kept his word and had some papers drawn up stating Alaye and his wife Aesimba otherwise known as Sunny and Sam were free to go wherever they wished.

"How long 'O Lord, how long," asked Sam as he began his every morning prayer, "befoe' we get to our great gettin' up mornin' and cross over that dark river to Beulah Land and we stands befoe' you an your throne? Lord I knows I'm jus a simple man and don' have much to show for all my years but could you look down on me an my family today as we go about our chores helpin' Mr. William get the cotton in? It would make him feel a lot better as he has been feeling poorly in his body for goin' on most a year now. Thas' about all this mornin' Lord and I'm thankin' you fo' all yo' blessins', Amen."

Prayers done he hurried as he put on his clothes consisting of a well-worn pair of beige homespun cotton pants held up by a length of rope and a one size fits all cotton shirt, which was followed by a pair of leather shoes with wooden soles as the original soles had long since worn out. It was late summer and he would not be getting any new clothes until the next spring. It was five AM as he rang the bell in the front yard by his shanty to wake everyone up to get started with the days work.

The overseer had died last year and Mr. William had asked Sam if he would take on the job until he could get someone to replace him. Along with the extra responsibilities would come a better house and better food. As he was already getting most of the food left over from the William's table because his wife was the big-house cook he couldn't imagine better food than that but he said he would take the job because of getting a better house; one with a wooden floor. Sunny, his wife was already at the cookhouse and the thought of hot biscuits and gravy made his stomach rumble.

Sunny smiled when she heard the morning bell ring, as she knew everyone would soon be coming to the cookhouse to eat. She had already been up several hours getting the brick oven hot because today was baking day, which meant bread, cakes and pies for the coming week.

Baking was usually done on Monday but it was harvest time for the cotton and that meant extra work for everyone, especially the field hands. She was very proud the day Mr. William had asked her Samson to take the job of overseer. It meant greater responsibilities for her man but along with it came a better house. She had even picked out a bright red-checkered bandana that morning to wrap around her slightly graying hair. This was the last day of cotton harvest and this evening all the field hands would come in from working the cotton and gather around a big fire in the middle of their quarters to celebrate. Mr. William had even said they could build a cook pit and roast a small calf, which he had bought earlier that week, just for the celebration. In her nightly prayers Sunny thanked the Lord for his generosity.

Mr. William wasn't like ordinary slave owners who beat them and always demanded more work. Instead he chose to share a portion of his wealth with his people. He never had to put a reward out for a runaway slave and her Sam never had to use a whip on a field hand to discipline them

Along with her job of house-cook she also helped Mr. William's wife in teaching the children some basic things to help them get along in the world. Before Mr. William had bought her a very angry man had owned her from South America who drank heavily but was very well educated and saw to it that she had some good education as well from a tutor for his children. He had named her Sunny because she always had a smile and a good disposition. She could both read and write.

Mrs. Claibourne had joined her in the cookhouse that morning. Sunny watched as she kneaded the biscuit dough and together they prepared the morning meal of pork sausage, cornmeal mush, biscuits and white gravy. Mr. William had given Sunny and Samson a milk cow as part of the extra benefits of temporary overseer so they would have milk, which had been hanging in the well, so it was good and cool. After the field hands had eaten and packed a mid-morning lunch of biscuits and sausage, she and the kitchen help would start baking before the heat of the day made it impossible to stay in the cookhouse.

Mrs. Claibourne had also told her about the visit her husband had made to a doctor in Memphis, last spring and found out he had brown lung disease. The doctor had advised William to retire and live a life of leisure in the time he had left, as there was no known cure for his ailment but he had decided to work even harder to make sure his family would be well taken care of.

Sunny had noticed Mrs. William often seemed in a daze and would quietly shed a tear sometimes as she worked. She loved baking and lately would be at the cookhouse, even before

Sunny, preparing the sourdough for the biscuits, much to the consternation of Mr. William.

After William passed away, Margaret found herself managing the plantation by herself, which was an arduous task. The cotton fields alone almost demanded her full attention. She was still a fairly young woman, and the field hands made the hard work a little easier, but she could tell in her body that she too would soon follow William. The plantation and cookhouse were heavy work for a woman and constantly being on her feet gave her varicose veins, which hurt almost constantly.

Soon a routine developed where she would arise a long time before the sun came up and gather the wood for the morning breakfast fire. Then she would prepare the morning meal; usually of yellow pan bread, potatoes and sweet onions, white creamy gravy, freshly cured sausage and mounds of sourdough biscuits.

As Margaret worked the biscuit dough on the kitchen counter with her strong hands, she reflected on her wonderful marriage to William and their only child who had died three years earlier. Silent tears ran down her cheeks and she wiped them away with the back of her hand. After the meal, the field hands would make sausage and biscuit sandwiches for a mid-morning snack as they left the house to begin the day's work.

Margaret died five years later.

Chapter Eighteen

Looking at the deed she could not believe what she was seeing, lease to buy, a plantation of the mid1800's with twenty acres of prime farmland for only $100,000 dollars. It was almost unbelievable but there it was right in front of her eyes, Rosewood Plantation.

She had only been in real estate a short time but she recognized a very good deal when she saw one. Of course, there would be the customary title search to be sure there were not any delinquent taxes or hidden surprises for the buyer later on. According to the information she had read, the plantation's original owners had moved from Atlanta Georgia and had lived at Rosewood for about forty-five years until their deaths at the ages of seventy-one and seventy-nine. After that time, there had been many owners but none had stayed for more than a few years and sold the property. This seemed very strange to Sarah. The plantation was only a short drive from Nashville so she decided to go see for herself if there was anything unusual about the place. The next morning she packed a light overnight bag, filled the gas tank in the car and made a mental check of any details she might have forgotten. Her Irish parents had taught her well.

There were many details and questions going through her mind on the road to the plantation. Why did the owners only keep it for a few years then sell? The original owners had stayed there for over forty years. Was it in so bad of repair that nobody wanted the expense of keeping it up? Maybe the place was haunted? A shiver ran up her back at the thought. Silly of me she thought. She had never seen a ghost, not that she did or did not believe in them, but she had several friends who had told her of things they had experienced. People in white wispy robes seemingly walking on air and going through closed doors or just standing there looking at them not saying a word, spooky stuff like that.

She had seen a few authentic photographs of ghosts or departed spirits as some people called them. She had never had the displeasure of the occasion in person, except that one time in that deserted old building that was scheduled for demolition. It had been an old hotel from the twenty's and thirty's and there were even a few reports of people being shot and strangled in several of the rooms. She had gone into the building out of curiosity more than anything else. She was very careful not to disturb any of the large rats who seemed to be the only residents as she slowly walked from room to room, not touching anything as there were spider webs everywhere, the dust was very thick on everything. In one room, she immediately felt a very cold draft as she entered and she could see her breath in the coldness as she took small quick breaths. Her pulse raced. She quickly looked around expecting something to come charging through the walls at her. Nothing happened so she quickly left the room and the building.

"No, Sarah Jean McCaffrey, you do not believe in ghosts," she told herself. Good lord, she thought, now I am even talking to myself. Next, I will be expecting to see the little people come running alongside the road. Still the questions ran through her mind as she drove. Soon she stopped in front of a massive iron gate. It looked like it could withstand an army. Beyond the gate, she could see a magnificent plantation style house, its white columns of Birchwood in stark contrast to the dark green trees and shrubs and many colors of the landscaping.

She looked around the large house and saw a well cared for garden; thousands of colorful flowers and roses in many colors. Small winding pathways wound through the garden forming circles and in each circle there were stone statues, works of iron that had been designed into umbrellas, archways, arbors and stanchions so that the hundreds of roses could climb on them. There were roses of all colors; delicate pinks, passionate reds, flaming yellows and pure white. The entire scene was something you might see in one of those old movies about life in the 1800's. She had no idea why she had stopped here or even how she had arrived at this address. There was a brass plate by the Iron Gate she read 1846. Suddenly a flash of recognition ran through her mind. She looked at the address for the plantation on her set of directions; 1846 South mill road, Lindbergh Tennessee. Somehow, she had driven through the small town of Lindbergh and arrived here at the plantation. She felt very strange about the whole thing, as if she knew ahead of time how to get here.

This had happened to her several times before. She would go on vacation and would see a shop in some town that she had never been in before. She would go into the shop and she would know the shop owner's name, and just how long the shop had been there. She also would know several names of the streets, and how to get around in the area, just as though she had lived there all her life. She reasoned that she had read somewhere about the town and had just memorized all the details. That explanation made her feel better about the experience anyway.

Well, no matter, she was here and that was the important thing; now to the business of finding out about Rosewood. She got out and opened the massive, finely tooled, black, wrought iron gate. She walked up the graveled pathway until she came to a fork on the path, one way led to the long wooden porch of the house, and the other led to the garden. She decided to try the house. On the porch, she saw two well- padded, very comfortable looking rocking chairs and alongside them, there was a swing suspended from two small chains hung from the ceiling of the wooden porch. The scene reminded her of stories of social family gatherings, ice-cold lemonade or tea in tall glasses and noisy children playing in the front yard and later watching fireflies, as the smell of honeysuckle and jasmine floated through the warm evening air.

She did not see a doorbell or door knocker so she knocked lightly on the door. A sudden shiver ran across her shoulders. No one answered so she knocked again. According to her information there was supposed to be a caretaker or grounds keeper on the premises. Maybe they were in the garden she thought. She carefully went down the wooden steps back to the fork in the pathway. She could not help but wonder at all the different varieties of flowers, especially the roses. Each bush or plant looked as if it had received personal attention. In the back of the garden, she could see a huge weeping willow tree. Close beside it was a stone bridge, which resembled an oriental pagoda. She stopped in front of one particular rose bush. It was huge. It completely covered a black, wrought iron gazebo, which was in stark contrast to the roses. They were small and pure white. Each rose perfectly formed. "It was his favorite," said a voice behind her. Startled, she whirled around and stood facing a lady who looked like a pioneer woman.

Her clothes looked neat and well kept but badly out of style. Like something out of the old western days; ironed white apron, brown bonnet cap, light blue dress with white ruffles at the wrist and almost brushing the ground as she stood there looking at Sarah from beneath her bonnet.

"Welcome home Sarah Jean," she said.

Sarah was thunderstruck. She sat down in the iron chair of the gazebo to collect her thoughts. It was almost too much for her; first the ride to the plantation through an unfamiliar town and stopping right in front of the gate. The shiver when she had knocked on the door, and now a mature lady who seems to have stepped out of the old west.

"How did you know my name? We've never met and what was his favorite?"

"Oh, but we have met Sarah. I am your great aunt, Jessie McCaffrey. I was there when you were born."

"Aunt Jessie? My mother spoke of an Aunt Jessie but that was a few years after I was born, thirty-eight years ago. That would make you…."

"Yes, very old."

"I didn't mean it that way; it just seems that you don't look that old." The more Sarah tried to apologize the worse she felt.

"You couldn't possibly remember what I look like," said Aunt Jessie, "After all these years and you were so very young at the time. It must be confusing so I will explain. Right after you were born, my husband Roger McCaffrey died, and all we had was this plantation that belonged to his family. It was the last wish of William Claiborne that the plantation is to pass down to the next of kin. You Sarah are the last of the line." Sarah thought about what Aunt Jessie had said.

"I don't think so," said Sarah, "according to the information I have about the previous owners William Claiborne had no children except Elizabeth who was killed as a teenager. So the line ended with her as there weren't any living blood relatives."

"You are quite right; Sarah, but William and Mary adopted a son right after the garden was completed, the same year that William died. They gave the young man their name but he chose to retain his original name of McCaffrey after Mary died. We are the last of the line, Sarah, and according to William's wishes the plantation is yours when I pass on."

"How did I know to get from Lindbergh to here and stop right in front of the gate?"

"Good question, Sarah, but we have always known things but we don't know how we know them. I am sure you have felt it from time to time but just not recognized it as a special gift. As for Rosewood, your great uncle and I have leased it out from time to time but it seems that the tenants do not want to stay for more than a few years. Such is the case for my being here now. The last tenants suddenly called and said they were breaking the lease, they didn't want any more of it."

"Aunt Jessie, is the plantation haunted?"

"Yes Sarah, I am afraid so. It seems that Elizabeth has not found peace and still walks in the halls of Rosewood."

"So the tenants leave because of Elizabeth? Does she go around moaning and making noises?'

"Yes, at times, and then she is silent for a long period. It seems she prefers to be active around the same day as when she was killed by that band of spies. Sarah…?"

"Yes, Aunt Jessie," answered Sarah.

"I fully realize that you have your own life and it isn't right of me to ask, but could you stay for a few days to help out a little. It is difficult to get up and down the steps anymore, and the garden is more than I can handle. A man would come through the area from time to time and work a day or so in the garden to prune the roses and keep the garden looking like it was planted yesterday. I ask as to the why of his work and the response is always the same, because of Mr. William and his generosity. You can stay as long as you wish, Sarah."

As they sat there by the white rose bush, Sarah looked around her at the surroundings. The previous owners and tenants had taken well care of the plantation while they were there. It would be a welcome change to her hectic lifestyle to get away for a while. She could still keep up her real estate business contacts here at Rosewood. The only thing she was not sure about was Elizabeth. Just then, a gentle breeze stirred the air. The long limbs of the weeping willow tree almost touched the ground as they swayed gently in the breeze. She took that as a good sign. She had a few small things to finish up in Memphis but she could do that and be back in a few days.

"Aunt Jessie, I would be very happy to stay with you a few days. I will need to finish up a few details in Memphis but I will be back in about three days."

Aunt Jessie was very relieved that Sarah had decided to stay. She gave Sarah a number for a Mr. Johnson in Lindbergh if she had any more questions. After many hugs, Sarah left Rosewood and went back to Memphis. On the morning that she was to return to Rosewood she received a call from Mr. Johnson, Jessie had passed away in the night.

Sarah was saddened by the news of Aunt Jessie's passing. She did not know anything about her great aunt but the short time they had spent there in the garden she had grown to like her. She supposed it was the way she had brought Sarah up to date on the family history and she had known that her time was very short and she had to be sure that Rosewood would be in good hands. Sarah decided to return to Rosewood but first she would spend a day in the library and learn about the plantation, the events around that time frame and she would find out about Elizabeth, if she could.

Chapter Nineteen

After spending many days at the county library at Nashville, Sarah found that Rosewood Plantation had a colorful and interesting history. It began in 1830 when a Doctor Andrews built the plantation. He married to Samantha Pruitt and they had a daughter, Evelyn. Soon after the completion of Rosewood, the Doctor sold it to William in 1846. Sarah discovered a curious fact about Rosewood; in the title search information made by William upon his purchase of Rosewood, he stipulated that any subsequent owner or lease person had to prove they are related to the Claiborne family line somewhere.

Rosewood Plantation was one of the most elegant and beautiful houses anywhere north of, what is referred, to as the Deep South. Four tall columns of Birchwood in front supported the huge verandahs of the second and third decks. The master bedroom on the second deck opened to a partially enclosed veranda. From there the view was magnificent. Down below was the circular, graveled driveway from the front gate entranceway and off to the left was almost a full view of the garden. The house itself had twenty-eight rooms, including three bathrooms on each level. The bathrooms were added as a convenience for Mrs. Gwendolyn Schmidt in 1904. Rosewood was sold in 1885 to the Schmidt's. That was the same year the haunting of Elizabeth began.

At first, they were passed off as settlings of the plantation, wind and animals in the attic, but then actual sightings of Elizabeth began to be reported. Mostly in the lower rooms at first and always accompanied by a very cold draft of air. Then after a while all the rooms were subject to a visit from Elizabeth. Her favorite trick was to turn the water on and off in the bathrooms. Almost like a child playing in the water. Another trick of Elizabeth's was to open the windows and shutters in the upstairs rooms, which was fine in the summer but often was a great inconvenience in the winter months. The Schmidt's would securely lock the windows when they would go out for a short time but on their return would find them standing wide open. It was even said that the Schmidt's took a liking to Elizabeth, as she never did any serious damage in any of her harmless pranks. In 1905, the plantation was sold to a family from Ireland and became known as the O'Neil Plantation. That same year Elizabeth took an interest in stomping on the wooden floor.

The stomping episodes began on October 20, 1905 and only in one spot; in front of the little door by the stairwell. They would usually last only about two minutes then would stop and not be heard again until one year later, exact to the hour and date; ten-forty five A.M. This continued for ten years. Then Rosewood and Elizabeth were quiet for approximately twenty years, which allowed the O'Neil's time to enjoy the beauty of Rosewood. Then in 1935, Elizabeth returned to Rosewood, this time her visits were different. Previously, her visits had been mostly unseen just felt or heard but now her visits were more physical and people had actually reported they had seen a young girl in her teens, dressed in a long, flowing dress. The dress looked badly torn and dirty in several places, beige or cream in color. Elizabeth would appear first as a light fog and take about fifteen seconds to fully materialize. She would stand at the bottom of the stairwell by the little doorway for a good minute then glide to the front door of the house, not making a sound. This proved to be too much for the O'Neil family. They put the plantation up for sale and after almost a year, it was sold to a Mr. Robinson of San Francisco.

Mr. Robinson did not believe in the supernatural nor did he support anyone or anything that did. He was a very wealthy shipping magnate and right away set about updating Rosewood. The walls were hand plastered and highlighted in rosette patterns and mosaics. The fine antique furnishings were resurfaced and polished. Many pieces were the original furniture bought by William Claiborne. The old staircase was rebuilt in fine mahogany wood and polished daily to a high gloss. Gardener's and landscapers were hired and once again, the townspeople of Lindbergh witnessed freight trucks and vans going through town and down the road to Rosewood. The Robinson family stayed in Rosewood about twenty years. Strangely enough, Elizabeth was not seen or heard during that same time until October of 1956.

In 1956, Elizabeth's visits became more regular; always at ten forty-five A.M. and always at the bottom of the stairwell. She would slowly materialize and then glide to the front doorway and then just disappear. The new owners, A.J. Conley, also reported that a dark stain just appeared one day at the side of the stairwell and no matter what kind of stain remover they tried on the spot it would not go away. They even put in new flooring in the hallway only to find that after about a week the stain returned. The Conley's knew that Rosewood was in all probability haunted but with the visits of Elizabeth in that same place and a spot that would not go away, their suspicions were confirmed. They quickly put Rosewood on the market and that was how Aunt Jesse came to live at Rosewood. In her search for information about Rosewood Sarah found out that the plantation came through the war pretty much intact, even though several major battles were fought just south of Nashville and to the East of Rosewood.

Perhaps the most one single act, which led to the civil war, was the Kansas-Nebraska act of 1854 and the raids by both sides in the Kansas Territory by both pro and anti slavery factions. In 1854, Southerners forced Stephen Douglas, Chairman of Senate Committee for the Territories, to repeal the ban on slavery as the price for their support.

Tennessee favored the south and played a major role in several battles in and around Nashville. The battle of Stones River, which took place Southeast of Nashville, was actually a union victory. The battle itself was fought east of Rosewood about fifteen miles. Union soldiers advanced east from Rosewood then took a south turn. Approximately forty-four thousand men under the command of General Rosecrans left Nashville on December 30, 1862 and proceeded southeast towards Murfreesboro where thirty four thousand men waited under the command of General Bragg. After three days of fighting and a combined loss of about thirty thousand men, it was declared a union victory.

While Sarah was doing research on Rosewood and the surrounding area during the Civil War, she found a small footnote in one of books, which stated that late in the war both sides had used small groups of spies to scout out the area before the armies would advance. One particular piece of information mentioned a plantation, southwest of Nashville that had been raided by union forces but not destroyed for some strange reason. The same note mentioned that two soldiers were found dead alongside the roadway about six miles east of the plantation. They looked as if they had been slashed and cut, probably from battle and had decided to desert rather than return to camp.

Chapter Twenty

During the next few months, Sarah kept herself very busy. She spent a lot of time in the library at Lindbergh. It was small but had a large micro file that she could access some of the other larger libraries. She spent so much time there that she was offered a part time job so she took it. In her research, she found that most of the furnishings were still there and had not been sold. Some of the pieces were originals; meaning one person for a special customer designed them. Their names read like a who's who; Alexander Roux, Mallard, Belter and Crouch.

There was the five piece set in the master bedroom made in 1842 by a French designer for a judge in New York and later was bought by William in 1844. It was valued at somewhere around $65,000. Many of the other pieces were equally rare. Like the French Rosewood Armoire, valued at $12,000, the seven foot tall wine cabinet with high detailed rose inlays valued at $16,000 and the Mallard Rosewood Etagere, reportedly made for a New Orleans Madam around 1860 so her 'ladies' could stand and look at themselves before going to their gentlemen for the evening. It was valued at somewhere around $11,000. Sarah was curious how it came to be here in Rosewood but that would have to wait until another time.

She had noticed another set of furniture in the downstairs sitting room. A five-piece set of rosewood consisting of two straight back chairs, two armchairs, and a love seat. A Henry Belter had designed it in 1842. They all were very well padded and looked very comfortable. Their value was somewhere around $46,000. Sarah struggled a little financially to keep up Rosewood but she made a promise that she would not sell any of the furnishings, something would turn up. She just knew it would and in the days ahead she kept herself busy dusting and cleaning.

One day as Sarah was trying to scrub away the stain near the stairwell she noticed a tiny, almost invisible crack in the wall. Upon close examination she could see it was a small door but had no handle or knob with which to open it. This was very strange she thought. Sarah felt around the edges of the crack seeking some way to open the access and as she pressed at the top edge the door swung open with the hinges squeaking loudly. Evidently it had not been used for some time and the small room smelled of mustiness and old dirt. Getting down on her hands and knees, Sarah went in.

The back panel of the space had a similar small door and as she pushed on the top edge it too opened to reveal a slightly larger room. This one had two sets of steps; one leading up apparently to the upstairs rooms and another set leading down into darkness. She decided to take the steps leading down and as she descended a strong, almost overpowering odor of dampness and dirt, stung her senses. She hesitated then taking a deep breath Sarah went down the steps. Thankfully she had found a kerosene lamp and some matches at the top of the stairs but its meager light did not help much to chase away the shadows that lingered in the darkness below.

Reaching the bottom of the steps Sarah raised the old kerosene lamp and looked around. What she saw caused her to take a sharp intake of breath! There were spider webs everywhere but as she looked closer she could see they had been deserted and not attended to in a long while. A fine layer of dust lay on each web and formed intricate patterns to match the design of each network of artistry formed by the spiders. As she stood there in the dark shadowy passageway she remembered something she had read a few years ago about plantation owners of the Civil War era were cautious and would often dig an escape route from the house.

Sarah had counted thirty steps as she had climbed down the stairs and estimated she was about fifteen feet underground. Keeping the lamp high overhead she started slowly walking, taking measured strides so she could estimate the length of the passageway. Someone had taken considerable time in building the tunnel. The walls and ceiling were completely covered with wooden planks and even though it had not been used in a long time the boards were straight and not warped from the dampness. Mixed in with the strong odor of dirt was a lingering smell of pine and she remembered termites did not like pinesap. In the dark dampness of the tunnel the only sound she heard was the fluttering of the small flame in the kerosene lamp. Realizing she had been holding her breath for a while she cautiously let it out and continued down the underground channel.

In the darkness ahead Sarah could barely see a ladder leading upwards. She stood at the ladder's bottom and counting her steps she calculated the tunnel was forty yards long. The ladder rungs looked to be made of metal and strong enough to hold her weight but she gingerly tested each one as she ascended the steps. At the ladder top she realized she had a problem because there was a wooden panel that blocked her from going any higher. One hand held the lamp and the other held onto the ladder rung so the only thing to do was push against the wooden panel with the top of her head. Dirt and straw fell onto her hair as she pushed and a small beam of bright light that shone through a small crack caused her to blink and close her eyes. Sarah pushed open the door panel and as she looked around she realized the escape tunnel led to the stable. Extinguishing the lamp and brushing the dirt and straw from her clothes and hair she closed the trap door and went into the plantation. She would explore the other steps leading upstairs in the little room another day

To help herself get used to the slower routine of maintaining Rosewood; Sarah would often take long walks through the garden, stopping to look at the many varieties of roses and flowers and to look at the statues and iron works that the craftsmen had gave so much of their time to build. Again, and again, she was drawn to the arbor and the iron bench on the heavy slab of stone. What was it about this particular spot that she liked so much; and what was it about the weeping willow tree in the back of the garden? Today she would enjoy the house and the front porch swing.

She got a small cover and a pillow from one of the downstairs bedrooms and arranged them on the old swing on the front porch so she could see the road in front of the house and the massive Iron Gate. She sat down on the swing, her feet not quite reaching the wooden floor. It was a quiet evening and there was no road noise to spoil the effect. The warm October breeze smelled of jasmine, honeysuckle and roses. She went over, in her thoughts, some of the details she had found out about the plantation during the war and the events that had happened to her since coming to Rosewood. Sarah sat in the old swing and slowly rocked back and forth listening to the crickets as they matched rhythm with the squeak of the swing. A few brave fireflies winked in the early evening light. She closed her eyes and drifted off to sleep.

Suddenly she sat straight up in the swing! Someone was stomping on the floor! She looked around but could see nothing. It was very late. The noise was coming from inside the house! Sarah set there in the swing, the cover pulled up tight under her chin. What should she do? What could she do? What she was not going to do was go into the house! Then the noise stopped. That was the loudest quiet Sarah had ever heard. She waited for a few minutes and then slowly put her feet down on the wooden porch and went to the front door. She hesitated, remembering the chill she had felt the first time she had touched the doorknob. This was utter nonsense, she told herself. She quickly turned the knob and opened the door, expecting to come face to face with Elizabeth, but the hallway was empty. The air was very cold and she could see her breath. Sarah flipped on the light switch and looked at her watch; ten-fifty at night. She was confused. According to Elizabeth's routine she was supposed to do the stomping in the morning, not at night. Had she changed her routine? Whatever the reason, Sarah would be ready the following year, should Elizabeth decide to show again. She went upstairs and to bed. She did not sleep well that night.

Shortly after Elizabeth's visit, strange things began to happen at Rosewood. Sarah would awaken, often in the middle of the night by bizarre noises, like leaves rustling in the wind and thumping noises in the walls. She would drag her herself out of a warm bed, arm her self with a big flashlight and investigate. As she checked out each room she would swiftly turn on the ceiling light and look around the room, nothing. Sometimes she would be very conscious of something, or someone, behind her and quickly turn around only to see a blank wall or empty floor space. On one occasion, she literally scared herself enough to faint.

Sarah awoke as she did before with some indistinct sound disturbing her much needed rest. She did her usual routine of turning the lights on in each room upstairs just to be sure that everything was as it should be. Only one room remained and then she could crawl back into bed and hope the rooster would forget about announcing daybreak.

As she touched the doorknob of the last room a violent shiver coursed through her body, she jerked her hand away. Slowly, ever so slowly Sarah turned the doorknob to open the door, a tiny bit at a time, using the beam of the flashlight to illuminate the dark space beyond. She could hear a rustling sound as she sneaked her hand inside to find the light switch and a cool draft of wind splashed across her hand. Finding the light switch, she quickly turned it on only to see a couple of very large rats scurry across the floor to escape through a hole in the wall. She looked and saw that a window was wide open; she reasoned Elizabeth was up to her usual pranks. The relief of not finding anything caused her to faint away.

Chapter Twenty-One

Sarah sat there at the top of the stairwell, her knees drawn up tight under her chin as she held her hands tightly against her legs. For the tenth time in the last five minutes she looked at her watch; ten-forty P.M. It was one year later from the time that she had stood at the bottom of the stairs and felt the numbing cold from Elizabeth's visit. She shivered at the thought. Again she looked at her watch, ten forty-two. She got up, and walked ever so slowly down the stairs and stopped at the last step. She stood there. This time the lights were on. She looked at her watch, ten forty-four. Maybe Elizabeth wouldn't show if the lights were turned on? Ten forty-five! Sarah looked at the area at the bottom of the stairwell where the stain was. A slight mist was forming there! Sarah watched in fascination as the mist swirled, she could see a shape taking form. It was Elizabeth.

She still wore the same soiled dress as before. "Elizabeth" Sarah asked. She could not believe her voice; standing there talking to a ghost. "Elizabeth," she asked again, "Can I help you?" Elizabeth was about five feet away and the air was bone chilling cold!

Sarah watched as Elizabeth glided over the hardwood floor and stop at the front door. She turned at looked directly at Sarah, and then waved as if for Sarah to follow her. Sarah could not move! Elizabeth waved once more then turned and vanished through the front door! Sarah walked to the front door and pulled it open;

she stood there face to face with Elizabeth. Elizabeth turned and looked at the front gate, and then she looked up and down the road as if looking for something. Then she turned back towards Sarah. In the light of the full moon, Sarah could see the features of Elizabeth very well, she looked so young and so very beautiful and in the moonlight Sarah could see tears on her cheeks, she was crying. In a flash, Sarah remembered there had been two deaths that day. Quickly she went around Elizabeth, down the front steps and down the graveled path towards the garden. She stopped and motioned for Elizabeth to follow her, Elizabeth moved down the steps. Sarah turned and almost ran to the back of the garden. She could see the pathway clearly in the light of the full moon. She stopped at the Weeping Willow tree, Elizabeth was right behind her.

Sarah motioned for her to look at the tree. Together they stood there, side by side. Around the trunk of the tree, a mist began to appear. A shape was taking form. Sarah could tell it was a man dressed in old-fashioned clothing; it had to be Charles! Except now, his clothing was not cut or torn anymore, and there was not any blood. Sarah turned to look at Elizabeth. Her dress was not soiled anymore either and she looked as if she probably did on that day before the soldiers came. Sarah watched as Elizabeth took one-step and took Charles's hands in hers. Together they stood there in the moonlight, facing each other, holding hands. Sarah could feel the warm tears on her cheeks. She was crying and her heart was very happy. She watched as Elizabeth and Charles walk, arm in arm, down the garden pathway in the moonlight. Then they just faded out of sight.

Sarah walked back up the garden pathway to the front porch. She stopped at the old swing and looked back at the Weeping Willow now nothing but a dark shadow in the moonlight. She had just helped two ghosts get together again after many, many years.

She cried some more as she remembered how Elizabeth had taken Charles's hands in hers as they stood there in the moonlight. It was getting very late and she was starting to get sleepy. She went upstairs and slept soundly. It was late in the morning when she woke up again.

Immediately she dressed in a warm housecoat over her nightclothes and went downstairs. At the front porch, Sarah stopped and stood at the top of the steps, looking at the Weeping Willow tree. Had last night all been a dream, she wondered? No, she told herself, it had been real! She had talked to Elizabeth and stood there as she and Charles had held hands in the moonlight. Sarah went down the steps and down the pathway as she had done last night. This time she stopped at the wrought iron arbor and stood in front of the Aimee Vibert rose bush. Elizabeth was already there. She turned as Sarah arrived and pointed at the iron bench on the heavy stone slab. Then she looked at Sarah and then disappeared. Sarah stood there, not knowing what to think. There must be something about the bench Elizabeth wanted her to see. Sarah knelt down beside the bench and looked it over, carefully. Then she got down very low and looked under the bench. Attached to the bench's underside was a small iron bar, held by two small clips.

Sarah unhooked the clips and held the bar in her hands, now what? It was far too small to move the heavy bench and she certainly could not use it to break the stone slab. She examined the slab more closely and found a very small slot at the back of the slab, right at ground level. She inserted the iron bar and pushed. The slab moved easily aside to reveal a compartment. In the compartment was a large, black, iron box that completely filled the hole. She reached down, raised the lid and opened the box. She sat there, stunned, looking at hundreds, perhaps thousands, of gold coins shinning brightly in the morning sun! This was what

Elizabeth was trying to tell her, to thank her for helping her to find Charles. Now Elizabeth could rest in peace at last.

Sarah realized she was suddenly very rich! Now she could stay here at Rosewood and take good care of it. What more could possibly happen to her, here at Rosewood?

Chapter Twenty-Two

Sarah had not ever seen an actual ghost face to face. She did not believe in them but the last six months at Rosewood lent considerable evidence they do exist. Sure there had been several times in her life when things appeared to be of the paranormal variety such as footsteps in the attic of a friend's house or a feeling you were being watched. One time there was an instance in a cornfield of one of her relatives that had been cleared for harvest. She had been walking along the road going out to the cow barn right at sundown and as she stood looking out over the field of corn stubble a breeze brought a powerful smell of decay and moldy dirt to her senses and caused a wave of nausea to beset her stomach and she immediately lost her lunch onto the dry dirt road. True she was on a farm and there were cows and farm animals that would leave manure deposits behind but this was no ordinary manure smell. It was of something that had been dead for a very long time. She reasoned it was no doubt an animal or bird. The last six months at Rosewood however, had been very trying and had badly shaken her non-belief in the supernatural.

The first episode started out fairly normal as she was sitting on the front porch swing. It was a warm summer afternoon, late in the season but not unbearably hot. The evening serenade of crickets and bullfrogs had not yet begun and there was a very nice light breeze to stir the air as she sat drinking a tall cool glass of tea.

She looked out towards the massive iron front entrance gate and saw several people coming down the road. There was something eerie about how they did not appear to be walking at all but sort of glided along on a fog surrounding the bottom part of their legs not making a sound even though it was plain they wore chains on their wrists and around their necks. A shiver ran across her shoulders and she almost dropped her glass of tea, which she was still holding up to her lips to drink.

Earlier in the spring there had been another incident involving the garden, which Sarah had observed but still had not caused her to accept a belief in ghosts. She had brought an overstuffed lazy chair from one of the sitting rooms downstairs and set it on the second floor verandah overlooking the garden. It had been an uneventful evening with the temperature around seventy-five degrees. The sun was just beginning to peek over the horizon through the cool air and already there was a blaze of orange, red and pink starting to filter through the clouds. She had chosen this spot as Aunt Jessie had told her it was William's favorite place to sit. It was starting out to be a glorious day.

As she sat relaxing in the comfort of the overstuffed cushions she looked down into the garden just as a wisp of fog drifted in from the backyard near the springhouse and into the garden. There was a good cool breeze that particular morning and was coming from only one direction, the southwest but the wisp of fog was stirring about as it moved against the breeze. It seemed to linger every now and then at several places in the garden and then move on and it was very curious because it moved only on the stone pathways. As the sun peeped through the morning clouds and warmed her face she glanced at the brightness and then looked back again into the garden. The wisp of fog had vanished. Later that day she went and walked around the area where the wispy fog had first appeared, near the old stone building. There didn't seem to be anything out of ordinary to warrant any strange activity. There was however a small pile of clothing in one corner of the small building, which fell apart when she attempted to pick it up. No bones or anything, just a pile of old rotting clothing. Perhaps the one single instance that had shaken Sarah's non-belief in the paranormal came very late one evening in the middle of the winter. It had snowed heavily the night before and there was a thick carpet of white on the ground as she looked out the front windows of the house. She watched as large snowflakes drifted slowly down in the morning sun. She decided to put on some warm clothing and take a long walk.

An hour later when she returned from her walk she looked at herself in the hallway mirror near the front door. Her cheeks were rosy from the cold but her features were very pale and had no color except the tracks of tears as they fell down her face. It was as if she was looking at a ghost, herself. The morning stroll had started out normal enough as she walked out the front door of the house and closed the gate entrance behind her as she began walking down the snow covered road in front of Rosewood, her breath frosted in the cold air as she took small strides, bundled up in her warm parka suit. The fur around the hood gently tickled her cheeks in the morning breeze. The air was crystal clear with only a few brave fluffy clouds to mar the blue sky. She lost herself in thought as she walked and after about an hour she found herself back at the gate entrance. There was a strong fragrance of roses in the air. This was totally absurd she told herself. It's the middle of winter. The heady bouquet of roses seemed to be everywhere as she closed the gate. There was just a hint of a wind and it was easy to follow the fragrance as it drifted with the breeze. It was coming from the garden.

A thick blanket of snow had covered everything during the night leaving behind white shapes of foliage that the summer before had been deep shades of green, yellow, red and gold. In the center of the garden she stopped dead still in front of the Aimee Vibert rose shrub. The fragrance was incredibly strong here. There was a single cluster of pure white blooms plainly evident even against the whiteness of the snow. There weren't any footprints around the shrub to suggest someone had placed the roses as a prank. Sarah looked more closely at the rose cluster and she could see it was attached to the shrub by its stem underneath the snow. As she stood there looking at the shrub she shook her head in disbelief. This was not possible. She reached forward to touch and see if it was real. As she touched the petals they suddenly fell off the rose stem and into her warm hand where they instantly dissolved as if they had been made from snow. She looked back at the spot only to see a blanket of whiteness as if the rose cluster had not even been there. Tomorrow she determined to explore the set of stairs behind the stairwell door leading upstairs.

The next morning Sarah debated with herself as she opened the door leading into the small space behind the stairwell, do I really want to do this? Silly question to be asking now, she told herself. Yes, she had to do this as her hand hesitated slightly before pushing the top of the second door leading into the room with the steps going up into the house. A shiver ran across her back as the stale air hit her face when she opened the small door.

The upward leading steps were easy to see in spite of the dim lighting so she decided against taking the kerosene lamp this time. The stairs were solidly built and squeaked very little as she put her weight on each one. There was even a handrail to hold and balance her self as she went up the dimly lit passageway. Sarah was thankful there were very few spider webs this time as some of the small ones looked to be occupied with tenants and hapless victims cocooned in small nets of webbing. Reaching the first level she looked around to see if there were any cracks in the walls to peek through and tell where she was. There was none. Evidently if there had been any they had been plastered over long ago. Feeling with her hands for an edge to push and maybe open a door panel she felt along the smooth walls and found a thin crack. Remembering the secret in the two small doors below she pushed at the top corner. The panel slid smoothly open on well-oiled hinges. She was in one of the bedrooms. Closing the panel she continued on up the steps.

At the next level there was an amount of light coming through a crack and she looked around the enclosure. Amazingly it was a fairly large room with stacks and stacks of wooden boxes. No doubt it had been used for storage, she guessed, but if it was used for storing things here, why not the attic as was customary with most of the old homes she had been in before. The box lids were all closed and did not have any locks on them that she could see. The lighted crack formed a three-sided pattern, which probably meant a door. This one had a doorknob on the side. She turned the knob and the panel opened to reveal she was on the second floor balcony. *What next? Do I shut the door and continue or stop here and finish the tour at a later time. I'll continue.* It turned out to be a bad decision.

At the third level she figured it was the loft and she was right. At the top of the stairs it opened directly into the flat floor space of the attic. The area did not have much lighting from the sun at all and as she looked around there were shadows and dark recesses in every corner. In most attics there were usually several vents to let the summer heat escape out and help cool the house but there were none that she could see and in fact it was not hot at all but slightly cool. True, it wasn't full summer yet but it was peculiar about the coolness. Her senses alerted as a faint whistle sounded behind her. Quickly she turned around but only saw shadows that seemed to dance. Sarah stood still so as to not make a sound and even slowed her breathing to short intakes. Nothing. Probably just an errant breeze that found a crack to play with, she told herself.

As she stood there the hair at the back of her neck began to tingle and a shiver ran down her spine. She could hear footsteps and they were not downstairs but here with her in the attic. She listened, all the while resisting an urge to get down out of the attic and into sunlight downstairs. The footsteps didn't get any louder which probably meant whatever was making them wasn't getting any closer to her. It was a full loft which ran the entire length of the house and she couldn't see all the floor space because of the many old trunks, boxes and furniture that had been stored up there for ever how many years. Plus the lighting wasn't the best either. Her senses were on full alert and telling her to get out! Sarah's breath was now coming in hurried gasps of air. The footsteps stopped! There wasn't any sound except Sarah's ragged breathing. Get out, now! With adrenaline rushing through her body Sarah scrambled down the three levels of stairs in record time and slammed shut the small stairwell door as she scrambled out into the hallway foyer.

Chapter Twenty-Three

Sarah awoke to rays of sunlight shining through the French lace curtains hanging on the brass rods above the beveled leaded glass antique windows. Rainbow prisms of light flickered all through the room and danced on the ceiling. Sarah leaned back on her lace edged pillows and stretched her arms over her head and for the first time really looked at the contents of the room. Up until now there had been so much going on she was tired in her body as well as her mind and she really hadn't paid much attention to her surroundings and simply fell into bed and tossed and turned all night.

The large canopy bed covered with French lace on the top was made of Rosewood, along with the rest of the bedroom furniture and had intricate hand carved design inlays. The bed was covered with a feather tick filled with downy goose feathers and the duvet cover had tiny pink colored rose buds. Across the room on the far wall was a fireplace overlaid in French picassiette mosaic tiles from mid 18th century, intense chalky colours; particularly blues, greens and pinks to the rich warm colours of Provence. The soft scrolls are influenced by French antique ironwork. Her eyes were drawn to it and she savored the beauty for a few minutes then moved on to the artfully hand carved molding at the top of the wall next to the ceiling and on to the breathtakingly beautiful Rene' Jules Lalique crystal chandelier which served as a reflector for the rainbow hues dancing about the room. It was too pretty to have been a guest's room.

This had to have been Elizabeth's bedroom. Sarah could almost feel her presence as she remembered last night how she had last seen them walking down the garden path, arm in arm from now till the end of time. She felt very happy and contented this bright new sunny morning as she arose and put on her bathrobe to go to the kitchen to brew a pot of coffee and make a few pieces of toast covered with homemade orange marmalade. As she came down the steps from the upstairs bedroom she noticed the stain had vanished from in front of the stairwell. The floor was clean and polished as if it had never been there. Strange she hadn't noticed it the night before when she went up to bed. Evidently with Elizabeth being reunited with Charles the badge of evidence signifying her lost innocence was not needed any more. As she sat at the small table in one corner niche of the large kitchen, sipping her steaming cup of hot coffee, she thought about the problem of ridding the house of those pesky large rats that she had seen scampering about in one of the other bedrooms. She was certain by now the family had expanded into aunts, uncles and cousins.

Just then she heard a faint scratching at the outside kitchen door and upon opening it she discovered a small fluffy little kitten; a calico with honey gold color along its back, white stocking feet and a dab of white at the tip of it's tail. Its eyes were almost an amber color. Light splotches of red and black scattered along its sides gave an overall effect of a rainbow of color. She gave it a saucer of milk and watched when it finished as it stretched and proceeded to clean its fur after the meal. Then it just curled up into a tiny ball on the floor and went to sleep. Sarah had no idea where it came from, or if it even had a home. She thought when it woke up she would let it out and see if it left or decided to stay.

With cats and their independent nature they allowed their owners to love them and there was no way of knowing at the moment whether it would find a home here at Rosewood or continue on its journey of exploring life. Actually Sarah hoped it would stay and solve the problem of the rats when it got a little bigger.

One morning as Sarah was sitting in the front porch swing, her feet barely touching the floor, a man came to the gate entrance and seeing her on the porch asked if he could come in and do some work in the garden. He explained it was part of the deal that had been honored for many years by the many men and their sons who had originally helped William to build the garden. Aunt Jessie had mentioned something about it the first day she and Sarah had met. The man had a fairly large and impressive array of tools in the back of an old pick-up truck parked by the gate. Deciding this was customary Sarah told the man to come in. As he went about taking his gardening tools from his truck and neatly placing them along the stone pathway in preparation to begin working he hummed a tune. The notes were very pretty and had a haunting tune reminiscent of old southern gospel brush arbor meetings. Sarah could not place the melody with any songs she knew but then she was only familiar with a few and not many of those were church melodies.

Every day for the next week he returned and worked in a different part of the back yard but Sarah noticed he paid particular attention to the Aimee Vibert in the center of the garden. She watched as he would take each group of pure white roses and gently prune away any brown or dead leaves. Such gentleness and care was uncommon with most men. There was something very strange about the man. The way he carried himself as he walked and went about working in the garden did not match up with the old dilapidated and beat up truck. Acting on pure impulse Sarah walked into the garden one day as he was working around the weeping willow tree and as she approached he stopped working, removed his leather gloves, turned towards her and said, "Yes, Sarah, can I help you?" She immediately fainted.

She awoke lying on the ground underneath the cool shade of an umbrella the man had acquired from somewhere. A cool wet cloth was on her forehead and a pillow from the porch swing was under her head. Her face reddened even more as she remembered how she had fainted when he had spoken her name. It just wasn't her nature. The man was sitting beside her on the ground with his knees folded in front of him. "How do you know my name," she asked?

"Actually it is quite simple, Miss McCafrey. Everyone in Lindbergh knows you now own the plantation and have been doing an excellent job of bringing Rosewood back to its glory days of beauty and splendor. My father's uncle told us when Jessie inherited the place and then when my father passed away it became my responsibility to keep the promise made so many years ago."

. I've been staying at the hotel in town while working the garden instead of the one in St.Louis so I can be near to work. I've never married and staying at the hotel is convenient for me"

"Can I ask your name?"

"Vibert, William Vibert. My great, great uncle designed the Aimee Vibert and gave it to Mr. Claybourne. I'm named after him and inherited the entire Vibert Corporation when my father died. Please excuse my arriving in that old beat up truck. It belonged to my uncle. I enjoy getting out of my suit and tie every so often, driving around in it and working the soil. Getting dirt under my fingernails helps to give me a sense of perspective."

The pieces of the puzzle fell into place to explain his gentleness with the roses. Sarah asked, "That first day you were humming a tune. I can't place the name of it."

"It's my favorite and it was also Mr. Claybourne's favorite. Shall We Gather At The River."

"Mr. Vibert, it may be very forward of me but would you like to stay for dinner," asked Sarah?

"Only if you will permit me to return to town, shower and clean up at my hotel and change clothes?"

"Shall we make it at seven?"

"Seven it is, Miss McCaffrrey."

In the weeks and months to follow that dinner at seven Sarah came to realize she was in love with William. They would often take long strolls, arm in arm, around the small pond some previous owner had made. There was a strong quietness about William that excited Sarah greatly. The way he spoke softly but with just enough authority that was not pompous or arrogant. Even though his hands were large and slightly calloused they easily held her smaller ones in their grasp as he would on occasion place a gentle kiss on each palm As they walked they would chat of such things as the relationship between his father, uncles and William Claybourne and how each succeeding generation would honor the agreement. It spoke well of a code of honor among pioneer businessmen that was often totally lost in today's hustle and 'quick fix' attitude associated with the younger generation.

On several of their walks around the plantation and through the garden William would chat about a certain area and tell her a quaint little story of something that had been passed down from generation to generation, father to son. Stories about gophers and their tunnels that appeared everywhere in the grounds surrounding Rosewood except in the garden and stories about the many rabbits, deer and squirrels that were seen throughout the plantation but very seldom were any of them observed eating the vegetation and flowers inside the garden. Sarah was not much on superstition, other than the 'Luck of the Irish' but it had occurred to her perhaps the garden had a protective angel looking over it.

One evening, two years to the day that she had helped to reunite Elizabeth and Charles, Sarah and William sat in the moonlight around a small table by the iron wrought arbor over the Aimee Vibert roses. Their garden dinner was a simple mixture of their favorites, broiled salmon cakes, broccoli and cheese casserole, a light Zinfandel wine and a small salad of lettuce, cucumber and tomatoes. It was a perfect evening. The garden was flooded with light from a full moon and they had been serenaded during dinner with crickets and katydids. Many fireflies courted each other with luminous flashes in the soft moonlight as they wafted on gentle breezes heavy with the fragrance of many flowers in the garden.

Then William reached across the small table held Sarah's hand in his and said,

"Sarah my dear, you've stolen my heart
And left in its place an ocean of love
A love so deep I will surely die
If you do not marry me and be my bride
This morning I saw a symbol of peace
In the form of a pure white dove
I realized then gold and silver mattered little
As I had found the jewel to fill my emptiness
I pledge to you the life remaining in me
A life of kindness, compassion and gentleness
And only in death will my love depart."

As tears filled her eyes, she said yes. The remainder of the evening the two of them sat on the marble bench under the Vibert roses.

"What of Rosewood after we are married," Sarah asked?

"We will keep it in the family of course," replied William.

On the evening of their first wedding anniversary William presented Sarah with a hybrid of the Aimee Vibert that he had developed. It was pure white with a thin rim of lavender around the outer rose petals.

Chapter Twenty-Four

Sarah tossed and turned all night trying to ease her mind from the events in the attic yesterday. It seemed that when she had something on her mind it just kept going round and round like some insane windmill without a solution. She couldn't decide if she was acting like a child or just being silly and letting herself get spooked over nothing at all. The footsteps, along with everything else that had been happening lately, was beginning to make her think maybe it wasn't her imagination. Sarah determined that she needed to go back up there and with a better light source and finish it, once and for all. She ruled out a kerosene lamp in case she panicked again and dropped it. A six or nine volt halogen light would do just as well and Sarah knew she should talk with William about having gone up there.

Maybe he would go with her this time. Sarah knew he had a pretty good sense of humor, who knows he might even like it. Besides, she knew she had to not only find out about the footsteps but what was in all those boxes as well and try to figure out who put them up there in the first place. It would appear that Rosewood Plantation still had many secrets and she wanted to know more of them.

It could very well be that some small animal had gotten into the passages and went up there, perhaps a raccoon or even some more of those pesky rats and maybe even Renegade could have been chasing the rats. He was still a little small to be chasing full grown rats but the experience would do her good. Of course it could also be another ghost or apparition but none so far none had been hostile, so what was there to worry about? Sarah made up her mind she would speak to William at breakfast in the morning.

It was a beautiful sunny morning as Sarah went out to the garden to pick some lovely Shasta daisies to put on the table. She went into the kitchen to put on the coffee and squeeze some oranges for fresh juice. She put the biscuits she had made from scratch in the oven and then started on the bacon and eggs. Not forgetting to take William's favorite marmalade out of the refrigerator for the toast. Outside the kitchen window Sarah could hear the morning doves and mocking birds singing their songs. Of course the robins were the early birds and were already hard at work catching their breakfast. Sarah believed in a good hearty breakfast to start a day off right. Renegade was sitting there on the floor looking up at her as if to ask what about me? Sarah knew that William had a very busy day planned so she hoped they would have time to talk and not wait until he came home in the evening. She could hear William upstairs humming his favorite song that she liked so well as he readied himself for the day.

Suddenly a crash upstairs nearly caused her to drop the pan of bacon. "William! are you all right?"

"Yes, dear I am ok, I just cut the corner too short and knocked over the clothes tree with my briefcase." Sarah thought that explanation a bit strange. As clumsy as she was she might do that but not likely that William would. Just then he came into the kitchen. "William, are you sure that is what happened up there", Sarah asked? "Sounds a bit strange to me." William had a sheepish grin on his face as he sat down at the table.

" No, that isn't exactly what happened," he said while sipping his juice. "It was probably my imagination but as I started to walk out of the bedroom I thought I saw a shadow pass across the wardrobe mirror and it wasn't mine. I turned to look and crashed into the clothes tree and knocked it over. I'm sure it wasn't anything. The window was open and the curtains were blowing a bit. The sun was shining in through the window and probably flashed in the mirror."

After William had left Sarah thought about what he had said for a few minutes and realizing William was not likely to imagine things happening out of the ordinary she rationalized that was the truth of it, or his version of it anyway. After all, a man has to have a few secrets. But, what about asking to see if he would go back up there with her? He had already left so it would have to wait until evening.

When William got home that evening he wasn't in the greatest of moods. It seemed to Sarah that he always had something on his mind and was easily distracted. She wished he would confide in her more about his business maybe she could help him to relax as sometimes talking about things helped to ease one's mind. She just felt there was something was just not quite right and she didn't have the slightest idea as to what it was. Perhaps in time he would open up to her.

After supper as they sat in the living room relaxing Sarah broached the subject of what had happened in the attic when she went up the stairs from the passage way. She told William how apprehensive she was about spider webs everywhere and the shadows dancing around as well as creaks and groans and finally the footsteps that came from the other end of the room. Sarah explained about the bad lighting and she couldn't really see very well anyway but she knew what footsteps sounded like and it was not her imagination. "William, I have to go back up there.

I want to know what is in all of those boxes and I have to know what caused those footsteps." In her mind though she wondered if it was possible that someone or something could have access to the house from the underground passageway but then it was plainly evident it had not been used for a very long time from the evidence of the dust on the spider webs. Even so it was not a comforting thought. "I would also like to check out the furniture that is stored up there and find out if it has any value and is worth keeping," Sarah said.

William was sitting in his favorite easy chair reading the evening newspaper. His glasses were resting on the end of his nose as he looked up from his reading and calmly looked at Sarah with a sheepish grin on his face and Sarah knew he was not taking a bit of it seriously. Well, at least he wasn't laughing. He said," it's worth looking into those boxes. How about we do it the first weekend that I have some idle time? The business has been keeping me so busy lately that I don't really have any free time to do much of anything that doesn't involve work. In fact I may have to start putting in some extra hours just to handle the load." Sarah sighed and said," Fine," but she knew it was not fine and he would no doubt forget completely about it in the next five minutes. Sarah also knew she would have to go back up there at least one more time, if nothing more than to check what was in those mysterious boxes. True, the business of those footsteps was really spooky and she could not rationalize what had made them but her curiosity would not rest until she had verified the box contents.

After William went to work the next morning Sarah sat brooding over a hot cup of coffee. William had changed his routine of giving her a hug and a kiss before going to work, two days in a row. True, it had not been much of a discussion or an argument last night but she silently asked herself, was the honeymoon over? Sarah decided she would go to the Farmer's Market in town and buy some fresh fruit, nuts and marshmallows to make an ambrosia salad. She had not made one in years and the thought of making one had come to mind last while thinking about Aunt Jessie. Sarah wished she had shared more time with her so she could have gotten to know her better. The last year had flown by so fast and so much kept happening that it seemed to Sarah she barely had time to think before something else happened. Something else indeed.

Chapter Twenty-Five

At the Farmer's Market Sarah walked through the many stalls and found fruit and stuff for the Ambrosia salad. It was very crowded, which was out of the normal for a Monday. God, she hated that word. Usually any day of the week is okay but there was just something about Monday that greatly aggravated her. It no doubt was psychological from her earlier days of being a working girl. As she strolled through the market she listened to the different sellers as they hawked their goods, each bragging they had the freshest and best to grace your table for dinner that night.

While Sarah was in town she stopped at a local detective agency and encored if they would undertake an investigation into the early deaths of Vibert men before their fiftieth birthday. Of course they asked a thousand questions, some of which bordered on personal information but she answered every one and the agency agreed to take her on as a client. However, their services were not cheap and she would get a weekly accounting of fees involved until she said to terminate the investigation.

On the way home Sarah stopped at one of the rest places along the highway to get a soft drink. As she sat at one of the concrete tables and sipped the cold bottle of ice tea she looked around at the way the rest stop was laid out. It had about a dozen tables; each was placed in the shade underneath a fairly large tree and each also had a small black metal stand in case you wanted to do some grilling. Sarah also noticed the rest stop had a walking path that led around the park and then off into the woods. Sarah didn't have anything to do at home except make the salad for dinner so she decided to take a walk. Putting the empty cold drink bottle in the trash bin she set out on the trail.

Sarah had always felt comfortable in the woods whether it had been just taking a walk like today, bird watching and photographing them, feeding the small animals or simply sitting underneath a comfortable tree and reading a book. Today she decided to take a few pictures as she always carried a camera, just in case the need should arise. It was just a point and shoot Canon LX with a zoom lens but it had served her well through the years and could be depended upon to produce quality pictures.

There was no need to hurry as Sarah walked along the path and she took a few pictures of red birds, Robins, Blue Jays and a couple of good shots of squirrel's as they chased each other up and down trees. It was a perfect day for hiking; the temperature was in the high seventies, low humidity and no smog to irritate your eyes like in the big cities. It was such a beautiful day. Sarah's thoughts lingered on that morning and William changing his routine of a hug and kiss before leaving for work and dismissed it as idle thinking which did no one any good. His business had been picking up a lot and she was amazed he could keep it all going without having a heart attack. He was a wonderful husband and more importantly she trusted him completely. It was still fairly early in the day so she decided to go back home and see what was in the boxes in the attic. The trip back home was uneventful.

Here we go again, she thought as she stood at the top of the ladder leading up to the attic. This time she had a halogen flashlight and with its powerful beam she could see every corner of space, There Mr. Shadow, take that and you, Miss strange noise,

I have a flashlight now. As Sarah shone the bright beam of light around the attic she was impressed at all the containers that had been brought up here for storage. She guessed the number to be around fifty. There were several old steamer trunks with rusty hinges and were covered with tourist stickers from all over the world; Sweden, Spain, Sidney, Belgium and Africa. She opened one of them and lying on top of the pile was a neatly folded white lace and brocade dress. Aunt Jessie's wedding dress. Sarah very carefully laid the dress aside and as she looked she found things someone had purchased as a memento of the trip; music boxes with small porcelain statues of dancers on top that turned as the music played. Old tintypes of pioneers, now badly faded, as they stood ramrod straight in their Sunday best.

As Sarah sat there and gently took each item from the steamer trunk she was reminded each precious item was a part of someone's life; a memory of good times shared with a loved one. One item in particular caused wet tears to flow down her cheeks; it was a light blue crystal cup and saucer heavily wrapped in silver foil. A barely legible hand written note was attached to the foil with a bit of ribbon, which read, an evening in Paris, June 1901. Sarah spent the remainder of the morning and well into the afternoon opening many of the travel trunks and wooden boxes in the old dusty attic and shed a few tears. Time passed quickly for Sarah and William and for the next few years. William would often take business trips to close some contract and he would take Sarah with him. It wasn't what you would call a vacation so they planned to take a lengthy one very soon.

It had been one year since William had passed away quietly in his sleep. They had celebrated his forty-fifth birthday in Australia that year and decided to stay an additional two weeks, as it was also their seventh wedding anniversary. Before leaving they had enlisted the services of Starnes and Goldman, a detective agency in

Nashville, to investigate why none of the Vibert male line reached their fiftieth birthday. When William and Sarah returned from their vacation they found a letter from the detective agency saying their investigation had found some interesting information and they would call as soon as they returned. There was two parts that William and Sarah wanted checking into; first was the mysterious early demise of the Vibert male line and the second was there a curse placed on the Vibert family? The second morning after they had returned, the phone rang.

"Hello?"

"Mrs. Vibert, excellent. Goldman here. I hope your vacation was exciting and uneventful. I realize our contract stated a weekly report but as you were out of town I will combine into one report our findings so far. The early deaths of the Vibert males were of natural health related issues and no foul play."

"And of the family curse?"

"That, Mrs. Vibert is the interesting part. I'll explain. Lewis Carver, made a deathbed confession in prison to placing a curse on the Vibert family because of Mr. Claibourne's choice to accept the Aimee Vibert for the memorial rose instead of the one offered by him, the Mme Zoetman of the botanical group Gallicanae, which he had no legal claim to anyway. Carver, it seems, was an occultist and practiced witchcraft. After Mr. Claibourne's refusal of his stolen rose he swore to place a curse and to ensure the curse would hold, in his perverted thinking, he killed an innocent man and buried him on the Rosewood property in the vicinity of an old spring house."

"Yes, I know where the spring house is located. Very close to the wooded area."

"Mrs. Vibert, I know a search team that utilizes cadaver dogs to explore an area for police work associated with missing people and corpses. If you will permit it I can contact them and see if they can find the remains."

"You may proceed but in the event any remains are found I insist they be released to the coroner for identification and then given a proper Christian burial where they were found."

"That is very considerate and charitable of you. I will make the arrangements."

"Thank you, Mr. Goldman. Please add any expenses to my account."

"Mrs. Vibert, concerning the private matter we discussed. Your concerns are groundless. The many meetings of your husband were all of a business nature and the long hours were all spent in the corporate building, either in his office or an associate's office, all male. I believe that concludes all our findings to date. Anything else I can do for you?"

"No, Mr. Goldman, I believe that will be all. Your services were very thorough and commendable."

Sarah was greatly relieved to hear the good news about her husband's long hours being of a business nature. In her heart she knew William loved her very much and was completely dedicated to his work. She was in such a good mood and it had been a wonderful day so maybe she could push her luck and make another visit to the attic without any unexpected visitors making their appearance and spoil everything. There were still a few boxes that hadn't been opened yet and her curiosity had not yet been satisfied.

Chapter Twenty-Six

Sarah's was sitting at the kitchen table finishing up her morning coffee when she heard the usual bumping against the outside door. She knew it would be Renegade coming home from his nightly visit with his ladies. She pretty much let him have his nights out as he always came home in the morning and scratched or bumped the door until she let him in. Oddly enough he never came home beat up or showing any signs of a fight. He must be the top cat in the neighborhood. She opened the door and to her surprise this time he was not alone. Renegade had brought one of his lady friends home with him and she was obviously swollen with kittens. It was just like him to go out and get his lady in a family way and then bring her home. Sarah giggled to herself, as it wasn't the first time.

Renegades lady friend resembled him in having mostly the same colors, white with black and brown splatters only she was a long hair. They were both wet and looked pretty miserable as it had been raining so Sarah got a towel, dried and fluffed their fur which did not make them Happy Campers at all. Then she gave them each a dish of food and water and sat back down to finish her coffee and ponder what to do with the remainder of the day.

As she gazed out the window at the rain she thought this would be the perfect kind of day to go back up to the attic and go through the rest of the trunks and boxes. It was no longer traumatic for her to go up into the passages and up the stairs. In fact it had become almost a routine by now. Sarah was familiar with the cobwebs and dust that usually left her sneezing as well as the squeaks and groans of the wooden steps as she walked up them. As she approached the attic doorway Sarah stopped. Stretched all the way across the top part of the door frame was the most intricately woven spider's web she had ever seen. For Pete's sake Charlie Brown now what, Sarah thought? She didn't want to get close to the web as she didn't have a great fondness for spiders but she could see the owner sitting stationary in the web's center. Laughing to herself, she stooped down and reached her hand up behind the huge web, opened the door and crawled in. Sarah just didn't have the heart to mess up the spider's beautiful handiwork. It wasn't a very big spider anyway.

In the first trunk Sarah found a bunch of civil war recruiting notices, circa 1861, some maps, civil war ladies bonnets, men's hats and a Confederate Uniform along with a pair of authentic Civil War era leather boots. There was also several Garibaldi ladies blouses, several dresses a few evening type dresses and some brightly colored aprons. In an old copy of Harpers Weekly dated February 1863 Sarah read about Murfreesboro, Savannah and the Army of the Potomac among other things and medals and a velvet bag containing a few coins. There were several Indian Head cent coins dating 1864 and 1865,1903, 1905, several 1917 buffalo nickels and many other Indian head coins. The number of buffalo nickels, mercury dimes and Liberty quarters boggled her mind.

In the next trunk Sarah found a Light cavalry saber, a civil war troopers sword and a Confederate staff and field officer's sword. She also found some handguns and with each one was a note explaining the guns history and whom they had belonged to. The handwritten note stated if there were any particular handguns used most by Union troops it would probably have been the Colt. The models favored were the 1851 and 1860 army versions, as well as the Starr revolver. For the Confederate troops it would again be either the Colt models or the Remington model 1858 revolver.

The note went on to say that large majority of Civil war soldiers; both North and South would not have owned a pistol or revolver, as these were not normally issued to the infantry. Revolvers, or handguns were mostly issued to cavalryman, and officers, whereas some of the artillery units may have had pistols issued for the gunner. Officers were issued handguns, or would sometimes buy their own.

Many infantrymen would often pick up a handgun they found laying around the battlefield, as they would consider it quite a prize. Pistols would often cost twenty to forty dollars so this was not an option, as many foot soldiers would hardly have one dollar to their names.

In among the stacks of boxes and trunks was a long flat case with the distinctive Sharpe's Rifle Company logo on it. Inside were a model 1859 Sharps, a model 1866, and an 1859 Sharps Carbine. In another case was a rifle made by Harpers Ferry Armory, circa, 1846-1855. Sarah was beginning to think this was quite a treasure trove and probably worth quite a bit of money not mention their antique value. On the bottom of the Harpers Ferry rifle case was a bowie knife. It looked quite authentic with its thick curved blade. On the floor beside the Sharpe's Rifle case were a couple of leg shackles and a folding pocketknife.

In the next trunk Sarah found some post cards from Murano, Italy specifically the Venetian Island of Murano where some of the most gorgeous hand blown glass in the world is made. Sarah, being a trivia buff recalled that Murano glass had been a famous product of the Venetian island of Murano for centuries. Located off the shore of Venice, Italy, Murano was a commercial port as far back as the 7th Century. By the 10th Century it had become a well-known city of trade. Today Murano remains a destination for tourists, art and jewelry lovers alike. Murano's reputation as a center for glass making was born when the Venetian Republic, fearing fire and destruction to the city's mostly wood buildings, ordered glass makers to move their foundries to Murano in 1291 and even today Murano glassware is still interwoven with Venetian glass.

In a small, brown, well used leather box Sarah found some post cards from Rome and the Vatican depicting Piazza del Campidoglio by Michelangelo, Fontana di Trevi by Nicola Salvi and one of the most emblematic examples of baroque art, The Spanish Steps. In the same case she found some old faded photographs of Ponte Sant'Angelo, the remains of the Appian Way near Quarto Miglio and Saint Peter's Square in Vatican City,

In one tourist pamphlet Sarah read the Villa Borghese, the 19th century "Temple of Aeschulapius" was built mostly as a landscape feature. Sarah had no way to dispute the validity of the information so she assumed it to be true. There were also several pamphlets from the Vatican showing the interior and the majestic wonder of Michelangelo's cathedral ceiling. There were also many informational travel pamphlets and post cards about Venice. One particular beautiful postcard was of the Piazza San Marco in Venice, which featured one of the many gondolas on the Gran Canal beside the Rialto Bridge.

In the next trunks were pictures of the city of amore', Paris along with post cards of the Eiffel Tower, which according to the inscription on the back of the photograph, was built in 1887 through 1889 on the Champ de Mars beside the Seine River. Recalling some trivia information about the tower Sarah remembered the tower was considered an icon of France and is probably one of the most recognizable structures in the world. In other pamphlets Sarah read about The Arc de Triumph in the center of the Place Charles de Gaulle or Star Square. The arch honors those who fought for France in particular the Napoleonic Wars and on the inside of the arc is inscribed all of the names of generals and the wars in which they fought. Underneath the Arc is the tomb of the Unknown Soldier dating from World War I.

There was one very large trunk that must have been Aunt Jessie's because there were initials of J.M alongside the lock hasp. In it Sarah found several bolts of French lace some white and some ivory in color. The lace reminded her of the curtains in Elizabeth's bedroom. She also came across the bill and shipping instructions for the Lalique crystal Chandelier that hung in the room. There were six assorted crystal atomizers to hold perfume of cologne as well as a white Opaline perfume bottle with Gold Ormolu. There was a pair of baluster form French Rococo style hand painted and gilt lidded perfume bottles with hand painted flowers surrounding all sides of the bottles in colors ranging from lavender, soft blue, pink, orange and a soft yellow with green foliate on white ground. All the bottles were still full of perfume and Sarah wondered why they had never been used. Mixed in with the assorted bottles of perfume was a bottle of Antique Guerlair Paris perfume. It was quite evident Aunt Jessie, or somebody, liked perfume. What wonderful trips that must have been to collect so many? Sarah envied Aunt Jessie a little and wished she had been the one taking the vacations and collecting all the postcards and souvenirs.

Sarah decided to take a little break and go downstairs and have a cup of hot tea. There lying in the corner was Renegade and his lady whom she decided to name Floozie. They were curled around each other and sleeping contentedly. As she sat there at the breakfast nook table looking out at the rain, she thought back on her's and William's trip to India to see the Taj Mahal.

Calling on her storehouse of information memorized from a travel guide about the Taj Mahal, Sarah remembered it was considered to be the finest example of Mughal architecture in the world as it incorporated a style that combines elements from Persian, Turkish, Indian, and Islamic cultures. It was completed in 1648 after twelve years of working on it.

During construction over 1,000 elephants were used to transport building materials consisting of translucent white marble from Rajasthan, jasper from Punjab along with jade and crystal from China. Turquoise from Tibet, Lapis lazuli from Afghanistan, sapphire from Sri Lanka and carnelian from Arabia and other precious stones were used as inlays in the white marble. In total, some twenty-eight varieties of precious and semiprecious stones were used

To do the work a labor force of some twenty thousand workers were recruited across northern India, including sculptors from Bukhara, calligraphers from Syria and Persia. Inlayers from southern India were also recruited; stonecutters from Baluchistan whose specialties were building turrets and others who only carved marble flowers. The stone cutting team consisted of thirty-seven men. According to the travel guide information Mughal Emperor Shah Jahan built the whole thing for his ladylove. The only souvenirs they brought back were some bolts of beautiful Indian silk, which were never used. Perhaps she would do that in the near future and make some dressing gowns or lounge pajamas. Silk always felt so good as it slid smoothly over the skin.

Underneath all of this were packets of letters. Each packet was tied with a different color ribbon, some had blue from Mr. Claiborne to his wife Margaret and some had pink from Margaret to William. Sarah sat there with the two large packets in her lap for a very long time deep in thought. Up to this point she had been full of curiosity and at times overwhelmed with the sheer volume of steamer trunks, leather valises and wooden boxes but now holding this last part of someone's secrets she was faced with the question; should she open them or not? Maybe just one, but Sarah knew herself very well and if she opened one she would have to open all the rest of them. Sarah hugged them to her chest as if trying to absorb the love within them. "No, Margaret and William, these secrets you can keep." Then she put the packets of letters back in the box and closed the lid. There were tears in her eyes. Sarah would not trespass on that which she felt did not belong to her. On the top of the packet of letters from William to Margaret was a hand written message:

We have seen the sights of wonder
The glorious days...the peaceful nights
We have touched and traveled deep into time
And beyond the stars

For we have loved and who could ask for more?
My love for you is not a gift to you.
It is a gift to me...
A heart full of love

Yet
No matter how much love it gave
For you there was always more

Chapter Twenty-Seven

Rosewood was slowly giving up some of its secrets. The attic had given up yet another good day of mementos, knickknacks, old love letters and precious memories. By now the routine was familiar to Sarah as she opened the small door at the bottom of the stairwell, put a fresh supply of batteries in the halogen flashlight and climb the stairs. The fourth trip to the attic turned out to be better than all the others although Sarah didn't think so at the time.. In one corner of the loft Sarah found a small, enclosed room that was locked with a heavy padlock attached to a thick metal plate across the door frame instead of the traditional doorknob and keyhole. As Sarah did not know of any keys that might open the lock, the only way to open the door was to cut the lock as the plate screws had been damaged to prevent being removed. Fortunately she remembered seeing a box of dust-covered tools along one wall, which might yield something to cut the lock. In the box was an old rusty hack saw but the blade still looked sharp enough to do the job and it was. In short order she worked the hacksaw and the lock was cut.

The heavy door of the attic room opened only to reveal a small, brown roll top desk covered with a thick blanket of dust and a single, very plain looking wooden chair. Sarah was disappointed. She had expected to find something of great value the way it had been safeguarded with the metal plate and lock. No matter, thought Sarah, just another mystery about Rosewood that might never be solved. The roll top desk did not have a lock so she rolled back the top and began coughing as the dust billowed around in the stillness of the small room. There was a single, faded green ledger book lying on the flat desk. Sarah opened it carefully as it looked to be quite old. The first page read Journal Of William Claibourne.

The journal's contents were just as much of a mystery as the little room with entries of the daily routine of running the cotton mill business, shipping orders to various companies and hundreds of notations to do with maintaining Rosewood; simple things like buying grain for the horses and farm tools for the field hands to do their work but nothing that warranted a high level of security. However, there was one cryptic note near the end of the entries, it read, three left, one right, two left, one right. It sounded like a combination to a safe or directions to get somewhere. Sarah shook her head, just another mystery. It was getting late in the afternoon so she went back down the ladder into the house, ate a light meal of broiled chicken, broccoli with cheddar cheese sauce, green garden salad and a small glass of chilled white Zinfandel wine. She rested peacefully the whole night through.

The next morning Sarah woke up feeling refreshed and full of energy, something that had not happened to often since William had passed away. Today would be devoted to light dusting with absolutely no moving of heavy furniture. As Sarah worked, she would stop occasionally and wipe a little sweat from her forehead before it dropped and marred a freshly dusted picture that she had taken down from a wall. Her routine was very simple; take a picture down from the wall, lay it flat on a desk, wipe the dust away and then hang it back on the wall. This worked fine until she came to William's study. It had two pictures on the wall. The first one was small and Sarah easily dusted it. The second one would not come down from the wall. It didn't look that heavy but no matter how much effort Sarah put into bringing it down the picture would not move. Remembering her early experience with the small doors she stood on a sturdy chair and searched around the top of the picture, pressing and pulling until magically the picture frame swung out away from the wall. Behind it was a black wall safe combination wheel, centered on a hinged square of dark gray metal plating. It only had numbers from one to ten on it. Remembering the cryptic numbers in the ledger; she entered the sequence in their order but the metal door did not swing open like most normal wall safes. Taking the door edge in both hands Sarah pulled back and then the metal plate opened to reveal only solid blackness behind it. There was no safe, only a thick blackness that had a horrible stench.

Well, there was no getting around it, she had to find out what was behind the wall safe. Finding a short footstool, Sarah stood on the top and peered into the inky blackness. The halogen light did not help much, as she could not see the far wall, which would indicate how big the space was. So she shone the powerful beam downwards and was relieved to see the floor about four feet below. Placing a well-moistened cloth over her nose and mouth and putting a bottle of water in her pocket, Sarah climbed into the dark hole.

She stood on the wooden floor inside the room behind the wall safe and shone the light around to get an idea of how big the space really was. It was only about ten feet square but the walls were not painted any color and looked like very dark wood, which explained why she could not see the wall earlier from outside. She couldn't explain it but the room felt very strong and solid. She stepped heavily on the floor a few times but there was no echo. In the beam of the halogen light she could see a dark square on the floor. Taking cautious steps she stood at the edge, it was a hole in the floor. Sarah flashed the light into the hole but could see nothing except a set of wooden steps leading straight down. Doesn't anything come easy with this house, Sarah wondered? She took the water bottle from her pocket and again moistened the cloth over her nose and mouth, and then she dropped the bottle into the hole. She counted about four seconds before it hit bottom. Well, at least it isn't bottomless.

The foul stench didn't seem as bad as Sarah climbed down the wooden ladder rungs into the hole. No, she was probably just getting used to it, she reasoned. She hoped the fresh batteries would last until she got back to the top. It was a very tricky business descending the steps with one hand and holding onto the flashlight with the other. Finally as she stepped down Sarah felt solid foundation beneath her feet. As she stood there shining the light around it looked like she had stepped into a large ancient Aztec store room The floor was solid stone as were the walls. Sarah estimated the room to be about twenty feet square and ten feet high. Gold and silver bars were stacked everywhere and along one wall there were large square strongboxes. They looked very heavy. On top of one stack of gold bars was a faded green ledger. Sarah opened the book and read some of the contents.

Ledger shipping and receiving log
Received:
January 1861
$125,000 gold bullion in coin from the Bank at Augusta
$40,000 in gold bullion bars from Bank Of New Orleans
February 1861
$300,000 gold and silver coin from bank of Danville Virginia
March 1861
$2,000,000 in gold bars from the bank at Louisiana
$200,000 in silver coin from the Savannah State Bank

$180,000 in gold and silver coin from Central Railroad Bank of
Savannah
Shipped:
March 1861
$2,400,000 to Richmond in gold bars and gold and silver coin
Received:
January 1862
$450,000 in gold bars from the Bank at Louisiana
$1,250,000 from the bank at Augusta
$250,000 miscellaneous gold and silver coin New Orleans
February
$110,000 silver coin from Macon State Bank
February 1862
$5,000,000 in gold bars from Dahlonega (C.G.M.)
$540,000 silver bars from Dahlonega (C.G.M.)
June 1862
1,500 ounces of gold bullion and 20,000 ounces of silver bullion
(Quilliam)

Sarah read the meticulously kept records and noticed there
was no record of anything being shipped in 1862 although there
were records of receipts for January, February and June. Nothing
was shipped! Sarah quickly scanned down the ledger total for 1862
receipts. The apparent total was over $7,000,000 not counting the
ounces of gold and silver from Quilliam. She looked at the gold
and silver bars stacked on the bare stone floor and the many
strong-boxes stacked along the walls. Could there be that much
money hidden here, Sarah wondered? Who did it belong too? How
was it brought here and by whom?

Sarah had to again moisten the cloth she had put over her
mouth to help her deal with the foul stench in the room. Why did
it smell so bad here? Money did not stink, not like this anyway.
There had to be a reason. She held the bright beam of the halogen

flashlight steady as she looked around the underground vault. The room was fairly large and completely walled on all sides with stone and mortar. Someone had taken a lot of time to prepare the space and the tunnel entranceway. In the back of the vault she could see an open doorway that led back into blackness. Just what I need, another tunnel, she thought. What I need is answers, not more tunnels.

Sarah carefully made her way through the stacks of gold and silver bars on the floor until she stood at the entrance of the doorway. She shone the bright shaft of light down the tunnel and just at the outer reach of the beam she saw a pile of rock and dirt. It looked like a cave-in had happened. Sarah walked down the rock tunnel and shone the light over the pile of rock and dirt. At the bottom of the pile a skeleton hand was sticking out from a piece of material. As she bent over and looked at the cloth she realized it was the sleeve of a decayed uniform, a Confederate uniform. Quickly it all made sense All the bank names in the ledger were Southern banks. William Claibourne, or somebody had been using Rosewood as a shipping and receiving point for the Confederate army. The tunnel had caved in, trapping the soldier or officer while either making a delivery or taking a shipment to Richmond. That only leaves the question of where does the tunnel lead behind the cave-in? Well, certainly the money didn't belong to her. Sarah decided to call her bank in the morning and let them handle the matter.

For the next few days there was busy activity at Rosewood. Sarah had called the bank and told the president of her discovery. At first he didn't believe her and said it was a very good prank but when she started naming the types of money involved, the different bank names and the dates, there was silence on the other end of the telephone for almost a full minute. Finally, with a shaky voice he said, "Mrs. Vibert, what you have discovered appears to be funds that were used to finance the Confederate army. Many of the Southern banks used secret holding points to facilitate speedy dispersal of funds rather than shipping large segments using conventional sources such as Wells Fargo. Mrs. Vibert, to be absolutely frank if the funds are as you say and were used accordingly, they could have conceivably changed the outcome of the Civil War. We will arrange to have the funds transferred to a safe holding place until proper authorities determine its outcome. Also Mrs. Vibert the reward or finders fee could be quite substantial. I will also contact the coroner."

"That would be wonderful, Mr. Levy. As for the reward or finders fee please set up a grant program for students going to college studying to be horticulturists. That would have pleased Mr. Claibourne very much."

"I will see that it is done, Mrs. Vibert ."

As Sarah hung up the phone she thought to herself. My goodness, I wonder how many more surprises and mysteries can one house hold. As she turned the corner she got her answer, there was Floozie and Renegade with their brand new kittens all five of them looking exactly like their Mom and Dad. What a nice way to end the day Sarah thought as she headed for the kitchen for a nice well deserved rest and cup of hot herbal tea.

Chapter Twenty-Eight

Sarah had been feeling a little uneasy lately. She wasn't sure why but perhaps it was going through all the memories in the trunks up stairs. Maybe it was time to get away for a while. Sarah really loved Rosewood and never felt as though she wanted to get away from it but just in the last couple of days she had started thinking about all the places here in America that she always wanted to visit but never quite got around to doing it. She didn't want to go alone and thought that just maybe Fannie her best friend might like to go with her.

Sam and Fannie Mendelson and their son Aaron owned and ran Mendelson's Grocery and General Store in Lindbergh. Certainly they would be able to do without Fannie for a couple weeks. Fannie and Sarah had become great friends and confidants after William's death. They had gone to Chattanooga once for a day trip for shopping and lunch and had a wonderful time. They often got together for tea and lunch either at the plantation or at Fannie's lovely home in Lindbergh. Every now and then when Fannie or Sarah felt the world was closing in on them for one reason or other they would go out to the garden at Rosewood and have a little picnic under the willow tree. They both seemed to be able to talk over whatever problems were at hand, calm each other down and resolve the problem.

There would be no problem with Sarah leaving Rosewood for a couple weeks since she had hired Lydia several years ago as maid and cook and general over seer to the running of Rosewood and taking care of the needs of the bed and breakfast guests. Lydia was a widow and had grown children of her own and Sarah welcomed her very competent help. She had made Rosewood her home, Sarah loved her friendship and it had taken quite a burden off of Sarah's shoulders to have the help and company. At first Lydia was a little hesitant about Rosewood and all the stories of ghosts and other things she had heard about the place but that soon passed and she soon adapted to running things.

After Sarah had spoken to Fannie she began to set the itinerary and get her things packed for the trip. She was really looking forward to the journey. They would leave the day after tomorrow. She thought first they would go to New York. After checking into the Hilton, Sarah and Fannie decided they first needed to have some lunch and they chose a New York deli. Coming in the through the door the first thing that hit their senses was the wonderful odors of dill pickles, corned beef and pastrami. Only in New York Sarah thought as her mouth was already watering in anticipation. Their table was by a window and Sarah was wondering where everyone was going in such a hurry. The sidewalks were crowded this time of day and everyone was walking in a head down manner and seemed to have a destination in mind. Perhaps they were on lunch break and still in thought from the morning business and just lost in their thoughts.

After finishing up their wonderful lunch they got a taxicab and headed to the Empire State building, which Sarah had always wanted to see and she was glad that they had an elevator because she certainly did not want to walk up all those steps. From their tour book they read that The Empire State Building is a 102-story Art Deco skyscraper in New York City at the intersection of

Fifth Avenue and West 34th Street. Its name is derived from the nickname for the state of New York. It stood as the world's tallest building for more than forty years, from its completion in 1931. The Empire State Building has one of the most popular outdoor observatories in the world, having been visited by over 110 million people. The 86th-floor observation deck offers impressive 360-degree views of the city and looking out over New York City and the view from there was enough to take their breath away. They could see for miles and miles as it was an amazingly clear day and it gave the illusion of standing on top of the world.

Of course Macy's in Herald Square was on the agenda as a trip to New York was just not complete without rubbing shoulders with a few New Yorkers to end the day and Macy's has been billed as the worlds largest store and has one million square feet of selling space, they also knew that Macy's put on the Thanksgiving Day parade every year. Both Sarah and Fannie picked up a few little items of lingerie and decided to call it a day. They were both tired and thought they would have their dinner in their room this evening and just sit back and relax and talk until bedtime. They wanted to go to Radio City Music Hall tomorrow and that would probably wrap it up for that day..

Fannie and Sarah both woke up quite early and were well rested and pleased that they had slept well even though sleeping in a strange bed, although they were very soft.. Sarah was standing over by the window looking out at Central Park and watching the joggers already into their morning regimens. Sarah mentioned to Fannie that she thought they should have breakfast downstairs in the hotel and perhaps then maybe take a walk in the park. Fannie quickly agreed.

As they walked along side the jogging path looking out at the lake and the ducks, both of them were in their own little world and were not aware of the man running up behind them. He ran right in between them and as he did he grabbed Sarah's handbag and sped up. However good fortune knocked and there was a fellow on the jogging path running right in their direction and he tackled the man. Sarah and Fannie both were shocked at the scene that played out in front of them and quite unnerved both of them. Things like this never happened around Rosewood or Lindbergh. There also happened to be a policeman on bike patrol and he came right to their aid. The policeman put the man in cuffs and radioed for him to be picked up. Then in the kindest way he could he reprimanded both of the ladies for carrying a handbag in the park. They thanked both the policeman and their savior and realized that they were no longer at home in Tennessee.

The taxi let the ladies out at Rockefeller Center on their way to Radio City Music Hall. The tourist pamphlet they got from the hotel said that the 12 acre (49,000 m²) complex in midtown Manhattan known as Rockefeller Center was developed between 1929 and 1940 by John D. Rockefeller, Jr. "Now this is interesting Fannie," said Sarah as she read from the pamphlet, "The Great Stage, measuring 66.5 feet or 20 meters deep and 144 feet or 44 meters wide, resembles a setting sun. Its system of elevators was so advanced that the U.S. Navy incorporated identical hydraulics in constructing World War II aircraft carriers; according to Radio City lore, during the war, government agents guarded the basement to assure the Navy's technological advantage. And The Music Hall's Mighty Wurlitzer pipe organ is the largest theater pipe organ built for a movie theater.

It was a wonderful show; they were thrilled by the precision dancing of the Rockettes, which are a tradition of the Music Hall. Their famous kick line started with sixteen women and now it has thirty-six. They are all between 5'6" and 5'10 1/2 and are arranged tallest in the middle and shortest on the ends. It had been quite an exciting day and both Sarah and Fannie decided to head back to the hotel and have dinner there. The service was wonderful and the food excellent, contrary to what the towns people of Lindbergh had told them before they had left," Those Yankees in New York just don't know what good food is. Save your money and don't go."

Sarah was beginning to feel very restless for some reason, perhaps it was being away from Rosewood for the first time in ages, or maybe the change of the hustle and bustle of the big city life but she asked Fannie if she would mind if they didn't go on to Philadelphia and New Orleans and just went on to San Francisco. Fannie said it was just fine with her she also felt odd being out of her comfort zone among all these people. Just too many crammed into one little space." The next morning they would head out to San Francisco and then on home.

It was the last stop on the last day of the vacation. Sarah was a little tired but she was sure a hot cup of tea would take care of that Fannie was also feeling a little taxed. There was just one item on the agenda for today and that was the Ferry Plaza, which was built around the turn of the century. Sarah dressed in casual tan slacks, Nike walking shoes and a dark brown blouse that had a small yellow flowery design, a light wind breaker as the morning was still a little chilled because the fog had not lifted yet. In front of their hotel they caught a San Francisco trolley car and after about a half hour they got off the trolley in front of Ferry Plaza. Sarah felt there was something very familiar about the building but she couldn't quite place where she had seen the building before. This was very frustrating, she thought. I can usually recall instantly information about a particular place but this one stumps me. Where have I seen this before?

Sarah stood about thirty yards in front of the Ferry Building looking at the structure in an effort to ease the feeling she had about the place. There was the clock tower in the middle of the building, the marquee out front, the twin sets of train tracks and trolley cars. As she slowly walked in front of the structure she stopped and closed her eyes. A cold chill shot through her body! But it wasn't a sense of foreboding or danger it was one mixed with love. Aunt Jessie was here! She opened her eyes and it was like she was looking at the old photograph she had found in the steamer trunk with the perfume bottles. The photo was of the Ferry Plaza almost completely faded away and in front Sarah could barely make out Aunt Jesse standing prim and proper in her Sunday best with a lacy umbrella draped casually over one shoulder. Sarah heard a whisper in her ear," Sarah, you need to go home now. There is business at Rosewood that needs attending to."

Sarah and Fannie immediately caught the next flight out to Nashville and paid the parking fee at the garage for her car and shortly after that she dropped off Fannie at her home pulled into the driveway at Rosewood. The mailman was just leaving and in the mailbox was a letter from the Lindbergh Bank. The bank president had returned the funds to the government and the reward totaled almost a million dollars. It seems the funds were indeed part of a system for transferring money from place to place and had it been utilized it would have made a vast difference in the war's outcome. There was also another letter from the detective agency inquiring if she wanted to hire the services of a paranormal group specializing in haunted houses. Sarah sent the agency a very nice letter and thanked them for their thoughtfulness but declined their offer, as she liked rosewood just fine the way it was.

Chapter Twenty-Nine

Sarah woke up the morning of her one-hundredth birthday to a bright sunny morning. Her window was open and she could hear the birds in the garden singing their happy tunes. At the foot of the bed curled around her feet lay the seventh generation of Renegade's litters. He had been a busy fellow. She glanced around her bedroom; which was formerly Elizabeth's, she always felt so happy and peaceful here with all its feminine charm. Everything was exactly the same as the very first day she had seen it. Sarah had purposely kept it that way having a feeling she would be back in it one day. She had three very special places that she loved here at Rosewood; the garden near the Aimee Vibert rose where William had proposed to her, William's favorite chair on the porch and her special place under the Weeping Willow tree.

After having a small breakfast and coffee Sarah walked through each room looking at it as if for the first time, running her hands over the furniture and stopping here and there, remembering something special about that particular spot. Although Sarah wasn't tired that morning she went out to sit in William's chair on the balcony before taking a walk in the garden.

As she sat in William's chair Sarah's thoughts lingered over her life and some of the events that had happened; the first time she saw Elizabeth at the bottom of the stairwell, the first trip to the attic and how could she forget the funeral for the young man who was killed by Vibert's rival and buried out by the woods. Sarah decided to take a slow walk out through the garden, as the air was especially full of many delicate scents from the flowers that morning Through the years she had kept track of that young couple that had first answered the bed and breakfast advertisement. They had moved to Nashville and had two children, a boy and girl and now had one Grandchild, a girl who was engaged to be married on her twenty-first birthday in four months. Her fiancé's name was Charles.

She was glad of her decision to decline any portion of the Vibert Corporation finances when William, her husband passed away. When he died everything was left for her to dispose of or keep as she saw proper but she said to divide it up in equal shares for William's brothers and sisters and their families. It had been many years since any strange events had happened at Rosewood and Sarah was very glad of that and she was sad at the same time. She had enjoyed a very full life and could not possibly have asked for more.

The next morning one of the guests found Sarah sitting underneath the weeping willow tree on the pillow she had taken from Williams's rocking chair. Her back was against the trunk of the tree, a blanket was tucked neatly around her legs and in her hand were two roses. One was the Aimee Vibert and the other was the one was the hybrid from it that William had given her as a first wedding anniversary gift. Curled around her feet was her constant companion, Renegade The Seventh and on her lap was an ornately carved wooden box containing Sarah's will.

The will stated announcements were to be made in the Lindbergh newspaper of her passing and notifications be sent to Mr. And Mrs. Finnegan and their only Granddaughter and that her will be read during the funeral services in Lindbergh. Rosewood was to be left to Elizabeth Finnegan along with all of

Sarah's inherited fortune from William Claibourne, as she had no known living relatives.

Shortly after the passing of Sarah Charles and Elizabeth were both killed in an accident involving a drunk driver coming home from a party and crossing over the divided line into their lane. Their daughter was not killed instantly but was so badly injured she lapsed into a coma and finally was removed from the hospital to a medical institution to receive care until she might recover.

As soon as the media splashed the news of the accident all over the state land offices started making bids and preparations for getting their greedy hands on Rosewood. All of them it seems had a legitimate claim to the plantation due to some long forgotten deed some relative had signed with them in the past. Legal suits were filed then counter suits until finally the state stepped in and seized the property for over due taxes. There the case sat for many, many years because no one wanted to step up and pay the huge amount of taxes that had accumulated.

With no one to take care of the plantation it quickly fell into a state of ruin and decay. Often cars would stop at the front gate and the passengers would get out and gawk at the shambles that once had been a showcase plantation of Tennessee. With no one to cut the grass and tend the flower garden weeds took over and soon choked out everything. It was almost as if its lifeblood had been drained and it no longer wanted to live.

The presiding judge over the case was tired of all the trouble that had been caused by everyone over ownership of the plantation during the previous years so he scheduled it for demolition the weekend before Christmas. Rosewood plantation however still had a surprise left and a young man named Jimmie Darcy filed a claim that he was the last living relative and entitled to the plantation and for another year the fate of Rosewood was in the hands of lawyers.

Chapter Thirty

Christmas fell on a weekend that year and at the last strike of the town square clock at Friday noon the judge's gavel fell with his verdict. "Be it as the plaintiff has provided overwhelming evidence to support his claim I rule in his favor." Jimmie could hardly believe his ears. He had won; the plantation was his and would not fall to the executioner's axe or in this case the demolition bulldozer. His lawyer, a quick thinking and hard working young man from Chicago had found a relatively obscure private domain property law dating back to the early 1800's. The prosecution argued bitterly and loudly but was ruled out of order by the judge and told to sit down.

At twelve fifteen Jimmie returned to his hotel and set up his antique computer which had made its grand debut in 2018 some ten years previously. At the time it was the best and fastest that money could buy and Jimmie being a computer geek anyway made it much faster almost enough to match a mainframe computers speed. His finger did not hesitate as it pushed the E on the keyboard to command the hard drive to execute the pre programmed job. In a split second the monitor flashed a series of lines across its screen to announce the command had been finished. Now it was in the hands of thousands of preservation societies, civil war restoration activists and newspapers throughout the country.

Jimmie had spent the better part of three years contacting civil war buffs, preservation societies and historians and asking them to support the purchase and restoration of Rosewood Plantation. Not necessarily because of its former beauty but for the part it almost played in the American Civil War. What if William's plan for helping to finance the south had been fulfilled? At that particular juncture in the Civil War it had been going very badly for the confederate armies especially after Shiloh and Gettysburg. Any kind of major victory after could have very well been the turning point in the entire war.

In an unbelievable short period of time after the request had been sent out letters began arriving at the post office in Lindbergh. Only a few at first then they came by the dozens and finally they arrived by the bag full and an area had to be set aside to keep them in the post office because Jimmie's small room at the hotel was already full. Each letter was from someone who cared about restoring things and making them beautiful once more. Some of them only had well wishes but most had at least a dollar or two enclosed. Of course the local banker was very happy to see Jimmie walk in the door with a fresh deposit.

As enough funds began to arrive Jimmie contacted a company that specialized in the restoration of old buildings. They had heard of the situation with the Rosewood Plantation and would be honored to take up the project. Their own chairman of the board was a Civil War buff and would be in close contact working side by side with Jimmie throughout the entire project. In quick time once again the road leading to Rosewood from Lindbergh was crowded with vehicles loaded with building materials except now the vehicles were trucks with flatbed trailers instead of horse drawn wagons. The massive wrought iron front gate squeaked loudly in protest as it was swung open to allow the dozens of workers to enter the yard. For a few minutes they just stood and looked at the decay and ruin that had once been a showcase plantation. A few of the workers sadly shook their heads and breathed a deep sigh because they knew the work ahead of them would require long and tiring hours but it was work they loved to do.

The roof was virtually sound and had only a few small holes caused by woodpeckers that loved the wooden tiles. The outside walls however were another matter altogether. As the crew began working they discovered termites had taken up residence in almost every board in the downstairs rooms. The underground storage vault was intact because of the cedar wood used in its construction. The once beautiful redwood furniture was now all ruined except for a few pieces in the upstairs bedrooms. Vandals had broken a few windows over the many years that allowed rain and snow to come in and form mildew and green mold on almost every thing.

In all the rooms cobwebs hung everywhere so the workers had to first clean out the spiders before any serious work could begin. It was slow work but taking one room at a time in a month the outside walls had all been replaced and also most of the interior walls. The floor had been oak and maple hardwood and although it had suffered some damage by termites it was easily repaired and three coats of oil and wax brought a luster back that it had not seen since William and Margaret had walked on it. As more money came in more crews were hired to restore the grounds and plant new grass. The garden was another problem however and it was saved to the last.

The bottom land that had been used for cotton and corn crops had long since been sold for taxes so only a small portion, six of its hundred acres were still listed as property of the plantation. The garden now lying in waste took up two of those acres and required two months by itself to restore. Horticulturists from practically every club in the United States sent workers and representatives to the plantation. Many of the clubs had records and photos of the garden in its former glory. The iron works were still there so it was just a matter of cleaning out the weed infestation and preparing the earth for new seeds, shrubs and plants. Even the weeping willow tree in the back part of the garden seemed to perk up as its branches were trimmed and pruned.

In a little less than two years Rosewood looked like a regal plantation of the old south around the end of the Civil War once again. At several times of the year a reenactment of a typical day at Rosewood was performed. People in costume played various parts and the public was invited to participate but most chose to sit and watch as the players went around doing their chores or trimming flowers in the garden, shoeing horses or putting hay bales in the barn loft. Some of the original acreage had been bought back from the funds that had been sent in and crops of cotton, corn and wheat were harvested every year to keep the plantation going. The shacks used by Samson and Sunshine had fallen down many years before and down below by the two rivers three small houses had been built and they were used by families that stayed on as caretakers year round.

After all the work had been completed and the restoration workers had left Jimmie took a room at the boarding house in Lindbergh and on any given day he could be found sitting in front of it in an old rocking chair. In front of him is a checkerboard he had set up on half of an old oak pickle barrel. Across from him sat another rocking chair and if you had time to sit and play a game he would tell you stories of his many generations past grandfather who sailed on the seas of the world.

In modern times people will argue that ghosts do not exist probably because they have never seen one. Even most of the residents of Lindbergh that have been there for many, many years will tell you they do not believe in ghosts. On several occasions, however, when the fog rolls up from the rivers, over the bottomland and covers the land around the plantation some have claimed they have seen shadows move through the mist and pause for a while and sit in an iron work chair in the rose garden and then move on down the road. Is Rosewood haunted? No one really knows for sure but if you happen to be walking down the road in the middle of Winter and see a wisp of fog lift over the garden and you smell roses…............?